GHOSTS I HAVE KNOWN
... and other true tales of suspense

CURT NORRIS

COVERED BRIDGE PRESS
North Attleborough, Massachusetts

Covered Bridge Press
7 Adamsdale Road
North Attleborough, MA 02760
(508) 761-7721

ISBN 0-58066-006-1

10 9 8 7 6 5 4 3 2 1

Contents

Acknowledgements

There are many friends I want to thank, and especially those who have shared with me the experiences of which you are about to read. My parents are at the top of the list. They were very tolerant Yankees, who like others of their vanishing kind, took other people and events at face value, never judging a book by its cover but instead relying on its contents.

They were objective writers as well, never interjecting their own opinions into their writing, but respecting their readers enough to feel that, presented with unbiased facts, the reader could his own reasoned decisions. My parents were liberal in the dictionary, and true, sense of the word.

Many of these stories appeared in my "New England Mysteries" column in the Quincy (MA) *Patriot Ledger*. I owe much to the editing and the friendly advice of Ed Querzoli, Terry Ryan, Bill Ketter, and a host of other *Ledger* editors. I extend the same thanks to Jud Hale and others at *Yankee* magazine, where several of these stories have previously appeared, and the same to Homer Jenks, formerly of the *Boston Sunday Herald*.

For my two sisters, Josie and Carol, and my late brother, Bill—thanks for being there. For their typing and editing skills, I owe much to Jackie Taylor of Brown University and to Dawn Trank of Wheaton (MA) College. And to my daughter, Katherine, for her final edit.

—Curt Norris

Foreword

This book is intended to be the first of a multi-volume anthology of true ghost, treasure, and other unusual New England stories. Although my true New England crime classics are reserved for another anthology series, the reader will find two true crimes included here which border upon the supernatural.

I have been personally involved with almost all of these stories. They are original and consist of new material which the reader will discover here for the first time. Some of these tales cross over into dimensions we cannot explain through today's technologies. Many of the strange events I experienced myself.

As a long-time science and medical writer—I was the first at the University of Vermont and also at Brown University—I have a scientific investigative bias that rejects finding a spook lurking in every dark and gloomy locale.

Nevertheless, I have witnessed events that absolutely defy logical explanation. One of my many fun assignments with the old Boston *Sunday Herald* was to spend a night in every haunted locale I could find in New England. My travels took me to some mighty strange locations, but I never witnessed anything out of the ordinary during this time of ghostly investigating.

All these experiences were personal. Many people have had an encounter with what they thought was the supernatural. Most won't talk about these experiences because they fear being mocked (as they probably would be, by the ignorant). I tend to believe that what we consider to be supernatural today will be explained logically a century from now. At that time in the future, scientists may have found out that indeed there are fifth and sixth dimensions, and that through errors of nature, time warps may occur. We consider these events today as unexplainable, much as our ancestors would have considered television and holograms ghostly a century ago.

At the moment, we must remain content with the almost certain knowledge that other dimensions coexist, which occasionally infringe upon the ordered, familiar and comfortable world we know.

Curt Norris
Norton, MA

Cape Cod's Buried Atlantis

An Atlantis is buried off Cape Cod. Unlike the original, fabled lost city of antiquity, the location of this submerged community is known. Few, other than some Cape Cod natives, recognize the story of the drowned town located off Wellfleet. Legend says it was the curse of a condemned man that sank Billingsgate Island. Others blame the anger of an Indian chief. Scientists would claim natural erosion.

Regardless, the island of Billingsgate was once the home of 33 families. It supported a whale-oil works, had a school, extensive oyster beds, and a lighthouse.

Now it is known as Billingsgate Shoal, marked at low tide by a few black rocks poking above the swells of Massachusetts Bay.

Cape Cod has always had its own magic, and in the unrushed mid-1930s, it was more genuine and less artificial than now. The characters immortalized by Joe Lincoln still strolled its streets and fished its waters. My family rented a cottage in North Eastham each summer and I remember, as a small boy, excitedly banging on the sides of our new Auburn car as we rolled over the railroad tracks opposite the North Eastham cemetery on Route 6.

A quick right turn onto a dirt road brought us to our camp, on the left, with Bert Whiting's land on the right. I was back there recently, but the area is heavily populated and consequently barely recognizable. In 1935 it was densely wooded. There were no neighbors save the many deer.

Every night in bed out on the porch, after the flickering lanterns were blown out, I listened to the Provincetown train wail its lonely way through the crossing below and then fade into the dark with a diminishing sound. I will always associate the smoky smell of kerosene lamps with those wonderfully peaceful days.

An old family friend, the now late Dr. F. Herbert Gile of Braintree, moored his cabin cruiser in Wellfleet. He added much to the pleasure of those summers. I remember the day he took us over to the site of Billingsgate Island in his boat. A black hulk poked jaggedly from one end of the sunken island.

"That's Billingsgate Light," he explained. "If you look over the side I can show you some stone walls and cellar holes where the houses once stood."

There was an enormous groundswell over the shallow water, but I staggered over to the side, and there were the ruins—deep enough under water that we could safely pass over them.

I was pretty excited over that discovery, but no one seemed to know what had happened to the community, which even today sometimes appears on road maps as "Billingsgate Island." I wrote to "The Answer Man," a popular radio program of the time, asking if he could discover its history. Eventually, a postcard came back with a note that "The Answer Man" could find nothing about Billingsgate Island.

As the years passed, fragments of the history of this local Atlantis found their way to me. Reading the books of Henry David Thoreau in college, for example, I learned that he had been a visitor there, and that an old fisherman told him he had as a boy seen cartwheel-sized cedar stumps just off the island.

Perhaps we should go back to the beginning. Legend tells us that Billingsgate was made into an island by an old Wampanoag Indian, who dug a channel on dark night, severing Billingsgate from the mainland. He supposedly remained noncommittal about his feat and so no one learned his motive.

Later—many years later—a Billingsgate native was convicted of a murder, and sentenced to death for the crime. Legend tells us also that as he was led up to the gallows, he protested his innocence: "If you hang me, so help me God, Billingsgate will wash away and disappear from the sight of man!"

In the 1880s Billingsgate Island was a thriving community located just off Jeremy Point in Wellfleet. Today, Billingsgate Shoal is a submerged sandbar, and the old building foundations no longer store potatoes and apples for a long, hard winter. Instead, they now support nothing but the sea life common to the shallow parts of the bay.

Billingsgate died a slow death. Her end was forecast by the lightkeeper, Herman Dill, who wrote in his diary, in 1875, "I do not know but what the island will wash away." He was particularly concerned about the high tides of that year which eroded a considerable amount of footage from the island.

The tides kept getting higher as the island got smaller. In 1882, the new lightkeeper, Thomas Paine, noted during one high tide that the whole island was covered, except a thirty-foot circle around the lighthouse. Time was growing short.

Gradually the residents left Billingsgate and moved to the mainland, until only the lightkeeper and the watchman who guarded the oyster company beds remained. In 1915, the lighthouse and the keeper's house were flooded, and the federal government built an automatic light on the eastern end of the island.

The last person to buy property on the island was a Boston physician. He used materials from the existing buildings on the island and built a hunting lodge, where he entertained friends. This idyllic life came to an end when the doctor's property dwindled to five acres, and he decided it might be wise to leave. The bricks he had used were salvaged and ferried to the mainland in 1922.

Billingsgate Shoal is now owned jointly by the towns of Wellfleet and Eastham. Neither town seems excited about its share of the sandbar and rockpile. Wellfleet owns the northern tip and Eastham the rest.

However, there are persistent reports of life of a sort on the old island. Every now and then eerie blue lights are reported to appear in the channel. Do the waters cover an unsolved enigma?

Did the Victim Become a Cat?

Hidden passages, windowless rooms with doors that lock from the inside, sliding panels, strangely slain corpses, ghostly figures flitting across neglected castle grounds, flickering signal lights and strange curses. All these traits were features of the Gothic novels that gained such popularity in eighteenth century England.

Despite the clever satire in the novels of Jane Austin, especially Northanger Abbey, *the genre captured the popular fancy and lasted well into the twentieth century through the works of J. S. fletcher and E. Phillips Oppenheim.*

Edgar Allen Poe not only introduced the detective story to the United States, but the Gothic tale as well, illustrated by his stories of the macabre, especially "The Black Cat." What follows is a true black cat mystery, complete with Gothic trappings. It involves a cast of transplanted New Englanders (who else could carry with them English customs?), a strange death, a bitter coincidence, and the seemingly human behavior of a stray black cat.

This tale is set in the unlikely locale of a modern (1908) and bustling Chicago. Austen herself could not satirize this tale—nothing is stranger than fact. No fiction writer would dare place his make-believe characters in the situations that confronted these very real people. All that follows was authenticated by first-hand sources.

Few people have died stranger deaths than Edward Darmythe, scion of an old Yankee family. He was shot to death within mere feet of his family, happily gathered together in their mansion, following dinner. He was found sitting upright in his chair, shot through the heart. No one heard a sound, saw any stranger, nor sensed anything amiss. Assistance had been but a few steps away at all times.

This was the situation confronting Chicago police on the night of October 27, 1908. And I have never investigated a stranger true crime. Darmythe was murdered in the library of his palatial home off Lincoln Parkway. His safe was robbed of a large sum of money while family members sat talking over the events of the day only a room away.

This is what they told the police: Following dinner, Mr. Darmythe left the parlor where he had enjoyed an after dinner smoke while chatting with his wife, son and daughter. He went into the library just across the hall, saying he had some letters to write. Behind the old gentleman stood a huge safe, the door ajar, exposing copies of business transactions and piles of cash. The son recalled that his father had opened the safe just before dinner.

Some time elapsed. The father did not return to the parlor, nor had any sound come from the library. Darmythe's daughter, Eunice, decided to check on him, because it was his habit to talk with the family across the hall while he worked. "Why is father so silent?" she asked her mother, who replied, "I suppose he is busy writing." Eunice thought he might be asleep, so she crossed the hall.

As she reached the open door of the library, she saw her father sitting upright in his chair, his chin resting on his chest. She nudged him gently and said, "Father, it is getting late." There was no reply. She looked more closely.

The girl's screams were heard by her mother and brother in the parlor and the servants in the back of the house. All rushed to the library.

The strangest feature of the crime was that the elderly gent had been shot through the heart and his safe emptied while his family sat only a few feet away. Through it all no one had heard a sound.

The authorities conducted an autopsy the next morning. They found a curious object in Darmythe's body, partly in the shape of a bullet and partly in the shape of a dart. It was about an inch long, with a very sharp point, and three flat, triangular sides. Experts believed it had been propelled by compressed air or electricity. Gunpowder could not have been used, and silencers for guns had not been perfected for use by 1908.

The mysterious murder of a prominent figure caused much speculation by the police, who nevertheless made absolutely no headway toward a solution. The investigation subsequently fell to Chicago police detective Clifton R. Wooldridge, a New Hampshire native and one of the outstanding detectives in the country at the time. He was told all that was known of the case, and given the death missile. From the meagre information the police had, he thought he had little chance of solving the mystery.

As the weeks went by without any leads, the news slipped from the headlines as the public found other sources of titillation. The case seemed to be an enigma, doomed to become another unsolved riddle of history. Then something so startling, so unusual, happened, that nothing in fiction could approach it.

A clue emerged through the actions of a stray cat. The following is condensed from the account of Preston Langley Hickey, a reporter for the old Chicago Record:

Late one night, more than a year after the murder, I met Detective Wooldridge while walking to my rooms after work. He, too, was returning home after a day at the police station. He suggested we walk home together and I gladly accepted. A cold and biting wind swept off the lake. With collars turned up, and hands shoved deep into our coat pockets, we walked along, mostly in silence.

We had covered several blocks in this fashion when I saw a large, black cat crouched at the foot of a corner lamppost. It was the largest black cat I had ever seen. There was something very unsettling about the way the cat was regarding us. It affected Wooldridge as well.

The detective admitted to me that he had always a secret fear of black cats, and were it not for my presence, he probably would have crossed the street to avoid the animal. This secretly amused me, for Wooldridge was a man of legendary courage. I told him the cat would probably scamper away when we reached it.

But the animal stood its ground. It remained crouched, and as we passed, it looked up and mewed softly. "Probably hungry," I observed. The detective made no reply. Our ways would part at the next corner, and we chatted for a few moments. As we started to leave one another, Wooldridge suddenly pointed back in the direction from which we had come.

"It looks like we have acquired a friend," he said. There was the black cat, following us at a brisk trot. When it reached the detective, it rubbed up against his leg and looked beseechingly into his face. Then it put one of its paws on his trousers and fastened its claws into the cloth, as though trying to pull him away. The detective bent over, unloosened the claws, patted the cat's head, and tried to shoo it off.

The cat trotted up the street a few feet, stopped to look back, and mewed loudly. Then it returned to Wooldridge and once again fastened its claws into his trouser legs. The performance was repeated several times.

"What do you suppose ails the animal?" Wooldridge asked me.

"Damned if I know," I replied. "I never saw a cat act like that before. It seems to be trying to get you to follow it."

"Perhaps it is. Let's see," said the detective, as he again loosened the cat's claws and began to retrace his steps. With its tail straight up in the air, the cat ran a few feet in front of the detective, trotting along as contented as could be.

I joined Wooldridge and we followed the cat for more than three blocks. Suddenly it turned into a vacant lot strewn with debris of all kinds—barrels, bottles, boxes, cans, and who knew what else. It looked like a dump. Wooldridge joked that the cat probably wanted to show us a litter of kittens.

About halfway across the lot, the cat stopped on a plot of soft earth and began scratching at it with its front paws, like a dog. Presently, having uncovered something, it stepped back, looked at us, and mewed. The possibility of the cat's having discovered a hidden corpse and uncovered a hidden mystery flashed across my mind.

Wooldridge lit a match and stooped down. With his free hand, he pulled from the ground a most unusual piece of apparatus. We took the object back to the sidewalk and held it under a bright arc light. At first glance it resembled a gun, yet it was different than any weapon either of us had seen before.

After several moments of examining the object as closely as he could under the circumstances, the detective fumbled in one of his inner pockets and appeared to put something into the strange device. A moment later he gave a cry of astonishment.

"Will you look at what I have found?" he exclaimed.

I did, and saw that whatever he had taken from his pocket fitted snugly and perfectly into the barrel of the weapon.

"What is it? Where did you get it?" I asked.

"That is the dart that killed Edward Darmythe," he declared. "And unless I am very much mistaken, this is the weapon with which the deed was done."

"How do you know?" I asked.

"For more than a year now, since I have been assigned to the case, I have carried that steel pellet in my pocket, more as a pocket-piece than anything else, I guess. Anyway, it fits this contraption and just as I know it is the bullet that killed Darmythe, just as sure I am now that we have the very weapon with which the deed was done."

We were in the 1000 block of North State Street, about a quarter mile from the Darmythe residence. It was 2 a.m. Despite the hour, Wooldridge suggested that we go there. As I started off to follow the detective, I turned to see where the cat was. It was nowhere to be seen.

There was a light on in the Darmythe mansion, so we mounted the steps and Wooldridge rang the bell. The door was opened by Darmythe's son, who recognized us at once. He led us into the spacious living room where a cheery fire was burning. A tall man of early middle age got up from a sofa and stepped forward. Darmythe introduced him as Edwin Manville, an old friend whom he had not seen in some time, and who had suddenly dropped in on him that evening.

"We have been reminiscing," Darmythe told the detective. "We haven't seen each other for several years. Manville is an inventor, and quite talkative." After general laughter, Wooldridge became serious and pulled the queer instrument from his pocket.

"Have you ever seen this before?" he asked. Darmythe shook his head and asked what it was.

"The gun with which your father was slain," replied Wooldridge. "I am not familiar with its mechanism, but it appears to propel the bullet with tremendous force by means of a spring or compressed air."

I noticed that Manville had perked up at the sight of the strange weapon, and jumped to his feet when "compressed air" was mentioned. He grabbed the gun from the detective's hand and asked where he had obtained it. A bewildered look had appeared on his face.

"Why do you ask?" Wooldridge said, as astonished as the rest of us were at the behavior.

"Because it's mine!" exclaimed Manville. "It belongs to me!"

"Yours!?" said the detective. "Well, then, it appears I have at last found the man who committed murder in this very house a year ago!"

"No," said Manville. "Don't be absurd. I did not commit this or any other murder. I mean to say that I invented this gun. It was my idea, and was made for me by a mechanic. He made only this one before he died. I had it made as a model."

"Then how do you account for it's getting out of your possession?" demanded Wooldridge.

"I sold it to a casual acquaintance of mine, named Henry Johnson. I think he was a collector, and he offered me a handsome price. I needed money at the time, so I sold it to him. This was two or three years ago. I don't know what became of him or where he lives now. I think I heard he went out West somewhere, and became quite wealthy."

"Well, if this isn't a coincidence, I don't know what is," said Wooldridge. "first we stumble on this gun, and twenty minutes later meet the man who invented it."

"Where did you get the thing?" Darmythe asked. So we told him the story about the cat.

"It sounds uncanny," Darmythe observed. "Seems as though the cat were guided by an avenging angel to betray the murderer, or at least give you a clue to work on."

Manville was on his way to New York, but promised the detective all the assistance he could provide, and added that he could be located through Darmythe. He said he would stop in Chicago as soon as he was finished in the East, if were needed.

"That's fine," Wooldridge replied. "I think we have a hot clue here, but we can't do much until Johnson is located. Would you know him if you saw him again?"

Manville assured the detective that he would indeed recognize the suspect.

Later, when we took our departure, Manville accompanied us as far as the corner.

"Now that we are alone," he said, "I have something to ask you. If it's not too late, would you accompany me to the Palmer House, where I'm staying? I didn't want to speak back there, and worry my friend further, but I may be able to help you further in this matter."

Once we were in Manville's room, he rummaged through the many drawers of his trunk, and then emerged with a triumphant look, handing a photograph to the detective of a handsome man of about 35 with wavy blond hair.

"This is Henry Johnson," Manville said. "It was taken about three years ago, when I sold him the weapon, and he couldn't have changed much in that time. You may have it. Now you have the gun, and a picture of the man who bought it."

When we left, Wooldridge insisted we return to the vacant lot to look for the cat. We found it, and he took the animal home, and kept it for years, until it died of old age.

The next day the detective went to the Harrison Street police station to study pictures in their rogue's gallery. It took him a week to go through it, looking for Johnson, but the effort was futile. The next step would have been to circulate wanted posters of Johnson to police chiefs across the country, but this never happened, because of another startling development in the case that made it unnecessary. Two weeks after the meeting with Manville, I received a call from Wooldridge.

"Something peculiar has happened," he told me. "Meet me at the Harrison station at seven tonight and I'll tell you."

At the station, he simply said we were going visiting. Then he hailed a cab and we headed for the Darmythe mansion. I knew this would be more than a casual visit, for Wooldridge was unusually quiet, and evasive about answering my questions.

When we arrived at the residence, we were informed that Edward Darmythe was in the library. As we entered, we found him in conversation with two other people, a man and a woman.

He arose to greet us, saying that the visit was a surprise, but that we were welcome.

"I hope so," Wooldridge replied solemnly. To me his tone sounded like the voice of doom.

I looked at him and found him staring at the other man in the room, seated by the young lady on the sofa. I followed his gaze, and barely stifled a cry of surprise.

"This is my sister, Eunice Darmythe," said Edward. "And this gentleman is—"

"Henry Johnson," interrupted Wooldridge, "whom I arrest for the murder of your father." The detective stepped forward.

For a moment we all stood, frozen with astonishment. The man flushed crimson to the roots of his hair, and then went deathly pale.

"Wooldridge!" snapped Darmythe. "This is Mr. John Francis, and my guest. Next week he is to become the husband of my sister!"

"Then your sister will marry your father's assassin," persisted the detective. "Whether he is John Francis or Henry Johnson, this is the man responsible for the deed. Here is the weapon he purchased from from Manville, and with which the murder was committed. And here is a picture the buyer gave Manville. Let him explain those things!"

"My God!" exclaimed Johnson. "Where did you get—" and then checked himself, and made a sudden dash for a open French window. Wooldridge, anticipating him, jumped across his path and struck him down.

Eunice Darmythe collapsed in hysterics. Two hours later, Johnson/Francis was stowed in the county jail, and Eunice Darmythe was in her home, under the care of a nurse.

At the same time, Wooldridge, Edward Darmythe and reporter Hickey sat in the office of Cook County state's attorney C. S. Deneen, as the detective brought the case up to date.

"The capture of Johnson was sheer luck," said Wooldridge, after explaining the black cat, the finding of the weapon, and the surprise meeting with Manville.

"When I failed to find a Bertillion record of this fellow (a precise system of measurements of suspects, used before fingerprint identification was developed), and no word came from Manville, I placed an order for wanted posters. But then I met Mr. Darmythe at the Union Station.

"He was with two other people, a young woman and a man, who had apparently just arrived. They were introduced as Eunice Darmythe and her fiance, John Francis, just arrived from Denver.

"I did not immediately recognize Francis as Johnson, but later, back at my desk, the penny dropped. To make sure I was right, I arranged with my friend Hickey, who had seen the picture of Johnson, to go with me to meet Francis. When I saw the look of astonishment on his face, I knew my guess had been correct."

The accused man was then grilled extensively by police, but refused to admit anything. In the meantime, Manville was sent for, and he arrived five days later. He positively identified the man as the buyer of the death weapon. The prisoner appeared overcome with surprise to see Manville. The next day, he was arraigned and indicted for first-degree murder. He pleaded "not guilty," as expected.

During the next month, the accused man refused to see or speak with anyone. And he made no effort to engage counsel. The court then appointed two young lawyers to represent him, but he refused their aid.

"I have no use for them, your honor," he told the judge. "I have ample funds, and if I wished legal aid, rest assured I could afford it." And there the matter stood. To all appearances, the man would go on trial for his life without legal defense.

Speculation about the case ran wild. Newspapers carried long stories; people talked on the streets. Some thought the man was crazy; others just shook their heads. But no speculation could be stranger than the truth, which came to light two days before the trial, when detective Wooldridge was summoned by the accused man.

He startled the veteran detective by confessing to the murder of the elder Edward Darmythe. He told the story as a man calmly relating the biggest mistake of his life. His real name was John Henry Francis, and he was from an old, respected New England family. He made Wooldridge promise to learn the facts of his life, so that the detective would know that this was the only blemish. Every step in the sorry business, he said, was coincidental. Nothing was premeditated. Here is the story he told:

He had met Edward Manville when they both lived in a Chicago hotel. Francis was a securities salesman at the time. A month later, Manville showed him the peculiar gun he had invented, and Francis thought money could be made from it. For the next two years, he tried to interest investors, but without success. finally, learning that a patent on a similar device had previously been applied for, he gave up. He continued to carry the weapon, loaded, on his person, but he really had no particular reason to do so.

Then he suffered financial reverses. A bad investment was followed by loss of his job. Things went from bad to worse. Then came the fatal day.

Going back and forth to his office, he passed the Darmythe house. Occasionally, late a night, he noticed an elderly man writing at a desk. Once, he saw the man remove a large stack of currency from somewhere behind the desk. Francis thought the man foolish for so openly displaying his wealth.

At about eight on the fateful night, Francis, worried about his financial condition, passed the house. Looking up, he saw

Darmythe inside, counting large sums of money. It was dark, no one was on the quiet residential street, and the French window to the library was open. On a sudden impulse, Francis darted in through the window, drawing his peculiar weapon as he went. Darmythe looked up, and the weapon discharged.

Francis swore to Wooldridge that he had not intended to kill Darmythe. In his highly nervous state he hardly realized the weapon had gone off; there was no noise and only a slight jar. But the sudden blotch of crimson on his victim's shirt told the story. In great fright, Francis grabbed the money on the desk and ran back out of the house. He later counted his haul as $8,000.

In his flight, he stopped only long enough to bury the gun, where it was later found by the cat. The next day, he checked out of his hotel and went to Denver. For weeks, he said, he did not look at a newspaper. He hoped he had not killed the man, but he was afraid to learn what had happened.

Before long, well situated in Denver and again solvent from profitable investments of the robbery money, he met Eunice Darmythe at a dinner party. Never having known the name of his victim, he did not know he was courting the daughter of the man he killed.

When he proposed and was accepted, his future brother in law asked that the wedding take place in Chicago. It wasn't until Francis arrived that he discovered the terrible truth. Not only that, he had to sit through a detailed recital of the murder. After a sleepless night, wondering what he should do, Francis steeled himself and decided to go through with the wedding. He would ease his conscience by by living a life of silent retribution to his wife and brother in law. This was the situation when he was confronted by Wooldridge.

He told the detective he was glad the matter turned out as it did, because he now realized he would never have been able to lift the load from his conscience.

The startling disclosures were published in all the afternoon Chicago papers. People thought he was crazy to put his head in the noose so deliberately. But Francis had puzzled over his situation for a month before confessing to Wooldridge. He had come to realize he could not live with what he had done.

Early on the morning of the day his trial was to start, jail attendants found him dead in his cell. He had hanged himself with his belt. On the floor was a brief note, addressed to Wooldridge:

"Is it not better this way?

The Bride in White

I don't remember my great-grandmother, Fannie Drisko Crane, but she must have been quite a character. In fact, I know little about the Cranes except that they left a library to Quincy, Massachusetts, and the Dalton branch makes quality papers, including the paper on which money is printed.

Fannie's family owned and sailed Maine coastal schooners, including shares in the *Hesper,* now rotting in Wiscasset.

Grandma Crane had a host of interesting friends, and among them was Henry Weston. In the family, the following story has been passed down through the years.

The Bride in White still haunts the Hall of Flags in the Boston State House. Once, thousands came to marvel at her beauty, but she is remembered by only a handful today.

Boston is a city of shrines, and among the more famous attractions of fifty years ago—and longer—are the images preserved in the Italian marble in the Hall of Flags, as well as in the foyer of the hall outside the Senate reading room.

Millions of people passed by, oblivious to these unusual rock-vein shapes created eons ago, until they were first noticed by Henry G. Weston, a Civil War veteran employed as a State House guide for many years.

While Weston was seated in the Hall of Flags rotunda one day, he discerned the form of a woman clad in bridal finery in the striations of the marble column in front of him. Later that day, he laughingly introduced her to a woman visitor as the Bride in White.

Word spread, and Weston began searching for other images in the marble. Eventually he made out several startling shapes. All would become well known.

Weston liked to compare the shapes to the proverb about "coming events cast their shadows before." Shortly before his death sixty years ago, he spoke with a Boston newspaperman:

"In this marble were buried veins which, when exposed by the marble cutter, assumed shapes that were not to become realities until thousands of years after the marble became rock. Yet these pictures are so true to life that they may be readily recognized."

The Bride in White, unlike other ghosts, needs much light before she blazes vividly forth as a beautiful creature with upraised arms. Her bridal veil reaches over her flowing hair down to the floor. Details of her gown are discernible, and once the figure is made out, it has a haunting beauty.

Weston liked to think that she was the soul of a mournful bride watching over the battle-tattered flag her lover gave his life for. His legend for her became famous.

The Athlete is just outside the Hall of Flags. Stare at him for a moment and he assumes shape. His muscles are tense, and he is poised for action. The tendons are distinct in his arm.

Another image is a perfectly formed English bulldog located outside the Senate reading room. The dog is complete with a wide, studded collar. An underslung jaw armed with protruding teeth lends him a ferocious aspect.

On the marble fireplace of the Senate reading room is a small hen with another chicken underneath her wing. Other images include the Naked Baby, the Balky Southern Mule, the Pig and the Rabbit. One of the most striking likenesses is of William Cullen Bryant, located in the lower part of a column.

The Kissing Cavalier is on the outer part of the marble stairway leading up from Doric Hall. Framed in its own panel, an Elizabethan-clothed cavalier bends over the hand of a demure maiden.

They are all there, yet the most famous was the Bride in White. She still wordlessly contemplates her lover's flag, and then silently disappears when the lights fade.

No one has shared her vigil in years. She is the forgotten lady of the State House.

Ghost of Bristol Notch

Back in the Reagan years, Washington gave permission for prospectors to begin explorations for oil and gas in the Green Mountains of Vermont. Unknown to many, this wasn't the first time the mountains had been attacked for their natural treasure. And because of some of these past events, folks around the Bristol Cliffs wilderness in Vermont become a little uneasy when they hear the nocturnal howl of a dog.

Under the high, brooding cliffs of South Mountain, a ghost dog and a boy guard an ancient buried treasure. Their vigil has been a long one. ...

In the late 1700s, an old man shuffled into Bristol. He ordered a supply of food in a foreign accent no one recognized and then disappeared into the woods.

A few days later, some boys came across the man prying among some rocks in the woods. He became surly and threatening when they questioned him. The frightened youths reported this to their parents.

The old man was soon visited by several angry fathers, demanding he explain his actions or leave the neighborhood. The old-timer unbent, but with reluctance.

His name, he said, was DeGrau and he was a Spaniard. His father had been a miner who had passed this way years before in search of precious metals. He had discovered a rich vein of silver and then left, returning the following year with supplies and a large party, which included the son.

They worked all that summer, hindered by wild animals and troublesome Indians, but managed to extract a fortune in silver. When winter threatened, however, they found they had accumulated too much treasure to move it all.

Near their diggings they found a cave shaped like a brick oven. They carried their treasure and tools into the cave, and walled up its entrance with flat rocks. They plastered mud and earth over the rocks, and a coat of moss finished the job.

The fortune securely hidden, the miners departed to their distant homes with the agreement that they would return the following year, and that no one would return without the rest of the group.

For one reason or another, however, the entire group was never able to make the return trip. The treasure seekers died, one by one, until only the younger DeGrau was left.

The old man told of cutting down alder trees at the river a mile and a half away, and burning them for charcoal for the mining operations. He mentioned two or three women in the party, one of whom had died. Her remains had been sunk in a pond a hundred yards west of the mine so that wolves would not dig her up.

After the Spaniard told his tale, the story spread around New England. DeGrau continued to search, scrape and dig. He stayed for a year or so, always hopeful. He thought the river to the westward and a string of ponds below verified the location of the old mine, but he finally became discouraged and left. He was never seen in those parts again.

Soon after he left, a strange and ancient vessel was found under a rock. It was identified as Spanish in origin, and caused much excitement in and around Bristol. There were people who, as recently as 1880, remembered seeing the jug, which could hold about a quart of liquid. It has since disappeared.

A flood of treasure seekers flocked to the area. Many of them followed the advice of the fortune tellers and clairvoyants so influential in New England in the 1800s. Others struck out on their own after the elusive silver—sinking one shaft here, another there. Hundreds of shafts were chipped and blasted out of the rock in the course of the next century throughout the area, now known as Bristol Notch.

Most of the shafts were dug in a similar manner. First the loose rocks were pried away, and a few feet were excavated into the solid rock. Then the digging was abandoned.

The Ghost Shaft is the most westerly part of the old workings, and goes down almost vertically for fifty feet. It then heads off horizontally for more than a hundred feet under the base of towering South Mountain.

According to local legend, a young boy fell into the shaft many years ago, and died before his plight was discovered. The bones of his faithful dog, who would not leave his master, were found above the entrance of the dig.

I have spoken with people who claim to have heard feeble cries and the howl of the dog near the site on dark nights.

Treasure seekers still visit the area, where, according to a long-ago visitor, "half an acre all around the surface is literally honeycombed with holes a few feet in depth, where generation after generation of diggers have worked their superstitious energies."

Much of that early work has been erased by landslides and dynamite blasts. But traces remain of broken hopes and wasted effort.

I recently visited this wild area of cliffs, ledges, holes, grout piles, and natural and manmade caves. To reach it, I had to travel down a lonely country road and hike uphill over rocks for about a half mile until I reached the base of he mountain.

Just as I got back to my car, a long, mournful sound followed me out of the woods.

Gert Swasey, Circus Queen

Every reporter has his favorite stories, those exceptional few that in one way or another have affected his life. I have covered my own share, and my father had his. This is a tale about one of his stories.

For six years starting in the mid-1920s, my father and Alton Hall Blackington were a reporter-photographer team for the old *Boston Sunday Herald.* Blackie was arguably the finest news photographer in New England, and his photographs are preserved today in the archives of *Yankee Magazine.*

During their adventures together, Blackie and my father became lifelong pals and mutual admirers. As I write this, I look over and see Blackie's two books perched on my reference shelves, each suitably inscribed and each containing personal—and biting—criticism about other well-known New England writers.

Because my father's papers are unavailable to me at the moment (they are at Brown University), I am going to write about a favorite story of the two men, that of Gert Swasey, the Circus Queen, paraphrasing Blackie's account in his *Yankee Yarns.*

One day in September 1926, Blackie was summoned to the Sunday editor's desk at the *Herald.*

"Blackie," he was told, "here is an assignment you'll like. I'm sending Norris up to Haverhill to get the life story of an old-time bareback circus rider. Her name's Wilson. She was with Barnum & Bailey and now she lives alone with a lot of cats and dogs. Go along and get some close-ups, and enough human interest stuff for a Sunday layout."

While my father went through the files in the morgue and returned with many clips on the circus queen, Blackie checked out his Speed Graphic and loaded a couple of extra 4 x 5 plate holders.

As the two headed for Haverhill, Blackie checked through the clips and learned that Gertrude S. Wilson was the only child of Moses Swasey, an old-time railroad man of means. A clipping from *Variety* was headed "Girl Saves Babe," and local clips told of the efforts of the Haverhill Board of Health to evict Mrs. Wilson from the three-room hovel where she lived with her many pets, which her neighbors claimed created a health hazard.

Arriving in Haverhill, my father asked a policeman where Mrs. Wilson, the circus rider, lived. The policeman replied, "If you mean old Gert Swasey, she lives upstairs in that shack by the B & M tracks, but right now she'll be washing floors in the depot."

Noting Blackie's camera, the officer added, "Better watch that camera. Gert doesn't like photographers—or cops. Last time I called on her, when one of her snakes got loose, she chased me with a kettle of hot water. She's tough, mister, and I'm not kidding."

Blackie shot a picture of Gert's shack, and just then she hove into sight. One hand held a pail filled with mops and rags, and the other hand clasped a broom. She wore a tattered trainman's cap angled over her gray hair and her yellowed teeth were clamped about a pipe, which emitted a cloud of smoke around her head. Gert wore a holed flannel shirt and a long, tattered black skirt. She topped off her apparel with brakeman's boots, which were much too large for her.

When she saw the two awaiting her, she put down her pail, spat vigorously, and said, "If you guys want me to pose with my pets, you'll have to wait until I change my duds. And look, if you put in the paper that Old Gert's going to give up her animals and live in the Old Ladies' Home, I'll bust the two of you right on the nose. Understand?"

At this point, Blackie said my father took off his hat and bowed, saying, "Don't worry, Mrs. Wilson. We just wanted ..." (Bowed? Well, maybe. He was brought up in a very proper Victorian home and had to address my grandparents as "mater" and "pater.")

"Don't you call me WILSON," she snapped. "My name's SWASEY. Daughter of Moses Swasey, the first man to bring a locomotive into North Station. God bless his old hide. As for that pip-squeak of a husband of mine, I hain't seen him since I kicked his hind end downstairs two hours after we was married.

"But don't stand there in the hot sun," Gert continued, "Come over to the house and see my little darlings."

When the "little darlings" heard Gert's heavy boots clomping up the stairs, Blackie recalls in his book, "they set up a chorus of yelps and howls that recalled feeding time at Franklin Park."

Behind the flyspecked windows, Blackie reported seeing "a dozen eager animal faces, and when Gert opened the door, she was all but knocked over by her furry and feathered friends. Cats of all sizes and colors rubbed around her legs, dogs leaped and barked. A parrot, minus most of his feathers, swooped onto her shoulder with an ear-splitting shriek. A mangy monkey curled a long black tail around her neck and with a vicious tug yanked the trainman's cap off Gert's tousled head and slammed it on his own."

Kicking empty sardine cans and half-chewed bones out of the way, Gert clumped over to her cupboard. She broke up a loaf of stale bread and scattered the chunks on the floor, poured some skimmed milk into one pan and put water in another.

"The room had been closed all day," Blackie wrote, "and you can imagine what it smelled like. We stepped out onto the 'roof garden,' a tiny square of tarred gravel surrounded by a sagging fence which was held up by stack upon stack of rain-soaked newspapers, magazines, and boxes bulging with last winter's ashes."

My father sat on what was left of a fine old haircloth sofa and Blackie found a good solid Moxie box.

"When Gert joined us, wearing a faded flowery dress," Blackie continues, "she flopped into a lop-sided rocker, hoisted her brakeman's boots onto a chopping block, beamed, and asked, 'How about some of your smoking tobacco? I gave up chewing ten years ago.' "

The two asked Gert how her day began, and between long puffs, she replied she got up around sunrise because she had to start scrubbing at the depot by 6:30.

"I work like hell all day, come home, feed my animals, and then from seven to midnight, I wash dishes in the dog-cart down to the square for my supper, and what scraps I can pick up. Folks say I'm crazy to bother with them," and she jerked her head towards the animals, "but I figure they're God's little lonely critters, and it's up to Old Gert to take care of them."

Just then a freight train hurtled by, shaking the shack and covering Gert and the newspapermen with cinders. Gert waved at the rear brakeman on the caboose and he waved back.

"I love it here close to the tracks," Gert said. "Takes me back to the days when my father was on the road. We had a big white house then and I had everything a little girl could want. You should have seen the playhouse I had, with a tower and an honest-to-goodness clock in it. Cost old Moses $2,000. He thought I had dolls in it, but I didn't. I had twenty-five sick cats and kittens I'd picked up, and I cured every one of them."

Gert said she never did take to school, but she sure took to horses. "I was the best damned rider in these here parts," she said. "I wanted to ride in the circus, but Moses said no. We had a hell of a fight over that."

On her sixteenth birthday, her father called Gert into the front parlor and said, "Gert, my dear, it's time you gave up these animals and got an education. I'll give you anything you want if you'll settle down and become a lady."

Gert stormed and swore, but her father won out. She was sent to Bradford Academy, and within two days, she had a pair of squirrels nesting in her bureau drawer and a skunk quartered in her closet.

She took care of pregnant pigs, removed burrs from the chin of an angry goat, turned cartwheels all over the campus, smoked a pipe, swore at the faculty, and smashed a violin over the head of the tutor Moses had hired to teach her to play.

Finally Gert found a way to get kicked out of school. She found that she would be expelled if she got married. Gert slapped her knee and laughed. She said it didn't take long to find someone willing to marry the only daughter of wealthy Moses Swasey.

"We was hitched at seven o'clock; ten minutes later we was fighting like roustabouts, and I knew I'd picked the wrong fellow. He had liquor on his breath and he tried to boss me around. Two things I won't stand from nobody! I grabbed him by the scruff of his neck, showed him the door, and said, 'GIT! before I break every bone in your worthless carcass! I haven't laid eyes on him since.' "

Moses was furious, but Gert reminded him that the two of them "couldn't trot in double harness" and he agreed, sending Gert to a second finishing school.

"All girls, of course, and the damnedest bunch of sissies you ever saw. They put chalk on their faces and chewed pickles so they'd have lily-white complexions. They made fudge, read love stories, and had sick headaches. I hated them! So I told Moses to get me out of there quick, before I busted up the place."

So Moses sent Gert next to his sisters in Peoria.

By this time, my father and Blackie were both becoming quite entranced and fond of this new character in their lives. They listened intently as Gert went on:

"Can you imagine me getting up at six in the morning to say prayers before breakfast? Them old maid aunts of mine made me practice on the piano all forenoon, then more prayers, a little dinky lunch, and tea and cookies at seven. Bible reading from eight to nine, and then to bed with all my windows shut tight. It almost drove me crazy!"

"And did you escape?" my father wanted to know.

"You're darn tootin' I did. I went down to the depot and made friends with an old colored man who cleaned out the Pullman cars. He wasn't feeling well, so I pitched in and helped him. I found some wonderful literature in those cars. A whole stack of *Police Gazettes* and newspapers from all over. One of them papers changed my whole life."

Gertie's face was aglow as she told of her escape from her maiden aunts in Peoria. "I found a copy of the *New York Clip-*

per and smuggled it into my bedroom," she recalled, "and that night I read every paragraph that had anything to do with animal acts or circuses."

On one page, she saw an ad:

WANTED: Bareback riders and female animal trainers. Apply in person. Robinson Animal Shows, Chicago.

Long before daybreak, Gert was up and out of the house. She found a man with a donkey cart and hired him to go to her room, get her trunk, and carry it to the depot. While the aunts were wondering why she didn't come down for breakfast, Gert was off on her great adventure.

It rained all that day and Gert was a mess when she reached the circus tents. The owner of the circus, John Robinson, was in the ticket booth when Gert announced her arrival. He immediately informed Gert that he didn't hire "runaway girls," and what made Gert think she could ride a horse, anyway?

'You old fool," Gert snapped, "I can ride any old fleabag you have, and there ain't a prettier figure than mine anywhere."

Robinson had to agree to this, but expressed shock at Gert's language. He put her in dry clothes, gave her a meal, and after her tryout, gave her a new career.

Gertrude Swasey soon found fame and fortune, her name in electric lights, and her face and "figger" on the biggest billboards in the country. She became the most capable and graceful of riders, the most daring, and a sensation.

As Blackie writes in his book, "Like a silver butterfly, she danced daintily over the smooth backs of four white horses, while they pranced around the ring, and she ended her act with a spectacular leap through hoops of fire."

One night her servant told her that there was an old gent with muttonchop whiskers, tall hat and carpetbag, asking for her at the ticket office. Gert realized that this must be her father, and asked that he be put in the front row so that she could "give him the thrill of his life."

"When Moses Swasey saw his daughter enter the ring," Blackie tells us, "all slim and shining in silver and spangles, he couldn't believe it was his own little Gertie who used to ride her ponies in the backyard ring at home in Haverhill.

"And that night Gertie rode as she'd never ridden before. To the cheers, yells, and whistles of the crowd, she came back and took a bow. Then, suddenly cracking her long black whip far out from the ring, she snapped her father's tall silk hat right off his head. It was the proudest moment of Moses' life."

In her dressing room, Gertie hurriedly changed to her street clothes, but the big tent was empty when she returned and her father had disappeared. A lump came into her throat, and for the first time in her life, tears spread over her face.

Wading in mud and straw, Gert tramped from one tent to another, searching up and down the midway. Then biting her lip and lifting her chin, she headed back to her dressing room.

She heard John Robinson yell, "Gertie! Look over at the side show." Gert looked and under the flickering glare of a torch light, with his silk hat over one ear and his sleeves rolled up, was Moses Swasey, selling tickets to a Hootchy-Koochy show.

Moses had bought the circus, "lock, stock, and barrel."

Both father and daughter were completely happy. Gert had found a place where she could lavish her affection on everything from the little white mouse that ran around the clown's hat, to Susie, the elephant who lifted her high above the crowds as the band played and the spotlights highlighted her act. Moses was happy too, for he and Robinson founded a great friendship.

One day, when the circus was playing out in the Midwest, Robinson's son visited the show, bringing along his baby, John Robinson III. Between the afternoon and evening performances, old John asked Gert if she could "rock him, or sing, or do something?"

Gert didn't like babies, but she knew someone who did—Susie, the elephant. Gert marched into Susie's tent, and said, "Susie, old girl, I want you to tend this bawling brat. I'm putting his cradle down here by your big, clumsy feet, and if you step on him, I'll whale the hell out of you."

Gert grasped the elephant's truck, pressing it gently against the cradle, swinging both to and fro.

"Now, not too fast, Susie. He's just a little tinker. That's it. Slow and easy. Keep your eye on him. I'll be back before the show starts."

As the sultry afternoon wore on, the animals became uneasy. A sudden shower sent people scurrying from the midway to the main tent while a rising gale tugged at the tent poles. Flags ripped from their fastenings, wires snapped, and finally the electricity failed and the lights went out.

The crowd surged towards the main exit, knocking down poles, stumbling over seats, and finally overturning three animal cages. One opened, and out sprang Nero, the lion. More afraid of the crowd than they were of him, the great beast slunk into the elephants' tent.

Gert was in her dressing room when she heard the alarmed cries. She pushed her way into Susie's tent, and stopped in horror. The elephant was still rocking the cradle, and baby John was asleep, but less than three feet away the lion stood, licking his chops and sniffing the cradle.

Blackie tells his readers that Gert seized a pail of water and flung it with all her strength into the lion's face. Then she scooped the baby from its cradle and cried, "Up, Susie, up!" Susie extended her trunk around Gert's waist and soon she and the baby were high—and safely—above the ground.

Gert told her visitors that afternoon back in 1926 that they should have seen the custom-built Pullman circus car she had.

"Cost Moses a pile of money, but it was worth it," Gert said. "He and I bunked in one end, and the stable was in the other. We always carried a barrel of rum and kegs of brandy. Every night after the show, I rubbed the horses down with rum and then covered 'em with two thin blankets soaked in brandy, with a dry one on top so they wouldn't catch cold. Made their coats shine like anything!"

Gert and her horses were well-known to the old-timers who followed Forepaugh's Animal Shows, Bostock's, and Barnum & Bailey's, from one end of the country to another. The old-time posters of Gert Swasey are very much in demand today by circus fans. This artwork shows her poised on tiptoe, on the backs of her beautiful animals. The tights she wears in those pictures were the first silk tights ever worn by a woman performer, and were a gift from P. T. Barnum himself when Gert joined the "Greatest Show on Earth."

Gert was paid $15,000 for her first season with Barnum, and $20,000 a year later. She spent it all lavishly—on extravagant living, on alley cats, mongrel dogs, and on any old trouper who was down in his luck.

Once she was traveling with a troupe, Blackie recounts, when the manager ran off with the cash box. The company was stranded and Gert came to the rescue, pawning her last family heirloom, a bracelet containing 145 diamonds.

George Primrose was a member of that company. Out of gratitude, he gave Gert his favorite horse, a real black beauty. When the horse, years later, ascended to horse heaven, she paid an undertaker to embalm him. And when her dog, Jasper, died, he was buried in a $75 casket. Gert sat on his grave for three days and nights so that kids wouldn't dig up the casket to sell as junk.

The years passed and Gert and her father traveled all over the country with various circuses and animal shows. When the old man's health started to fail, they limited their travels to Boston and New York, where they played twice a year, at Madison Square Garden and at the old Huntington Avenue circus grounds.

Finally Moses became bed-ridden, so Gert Swasey stayed home to tend him and the dozen or so stray cats and dogs she picked up around the neighborhood. After her father died, the estate, the big white house, and a sizable sum of money were tied up and dissipated in a long and bitter litigation.

Gert was flat broke. To get food for herself and her animals, she washed dishes in a restaurant and scrubbed floors at the depot, and moved into the three-room shack where Blackie and my father found her.

As the two newspapermen left, they looked into the open window of the cluttered "kitchen" and noted on the wall a faded, fly-specked poster. It showed a wasp-waisted damsel in silk tights and spangles, poised on the back of a prancing steed and framed by hoops of fire.

It was Gert, Blackie writes, in her prime as a circus rider.

"Seven years later, in December 1933," Blackie writes, "something strange happened."

"It was cold and wet and windy, and early Christmas shoppers held their ears as they braved the biting winds on Tremont Street in Boston. The store windows, tinged with frost, sparkled with tinsel and colored lights—there was the sound of Christmas, also, with tinkling toys and children."

Suddenly it made Blackie think of a circus and the thought occurred to him, "Whatever became of that old woman up in Haverhill? The circus queen? What was her name? Gert Swasey!"

Blackie hurried to his office, and tried to dictate some letters. But now the "voice" insisted that Blackie go to Haverhill and see how old Gert was getting along. He grabbed his assistant and the two left for Haverhill.

Car heaters weren't so good back in '33 and the two thought they would freeze before they reached Haverhill and Gert's old shack. But they made it, and Blackie noted that Gert's shack was more rundown than ever. No smoke came from the lopsided chimney and there were no tracks on the snow-covered stairway. They climbed the sagging stairs and knocked on the door. There was no answer, no barking of dogs, and Blackie pushed the door open.

The kitchen was cold and empty and the winter winds howled through the broken windows, not quite well enough stuffed with old rags and old newspapers. Snow had sneaked under the door and the wallpaper was gone, including the old poster (called a "one sheet" in Gert's time) of Gert as a bareback rider.

Outside of a rusty stove, supported at one corner by a brick, there wasn't a stick of furniture. The sink faucet was covered with icicles. Rusty water from a broken pipe oozed over the muddy floor. In the next room, Blackie and his assistant noted the flame of an old "fishtail" gas burner. Blackie turned up the gas and found Gert.

She was on the floor, on an old feather mattress, in a pile of bedding, breathing hard and clutching a small dead dog to her breast. Blackie sent George out for some hot soup, hot coffee and anything else he could think of. Blackie lifted Gert to a half-sitting position with her back against the wall. She wore an old topcoat, held together with nails for buttons and a rope tied about her waist.

She still wore brakeman's boots and long strands of hair hung down over her face, but her eyes were bright as she smiled and whispered, "Thank God you've come, Moses! You got here just in time!" Then she looked again and said, "You ain't my father. Who the hell are you?"

"Santa Claus," Blackie answered. Her next words were familiar.

"Have you got any smoking terbacca?" Then she said, "Do you believe in spirits?"

"Sure. Why?"

"Moses' spirit was here last night. I was lying in the corner under the rags and I seen a bright light, just like the headlight on his locomotive, and there he stood big as life. But when I put my hands out to him, he shook his head and said, 'Not tonight Gertie, tomorrow. I'll come tomorrow sure and bring you something to eat.'"

Gert pawed at tears that gathered in her eyes. "He couldn't come himself, so he sent you instead."

Blackie looked around for something to start a fire with and found plenty of kindling and a bathtub full of coal. Gert had no use for the tub and she had forgotten about the fuel. In the boarded up back room, Blackie found the old horsehair sofa that my father had sat on during the 1926 interview. When George returned with blankets and food, the two brought out the sofa and lifted Gert onto it. They then said good-bye and headed back to Boston.

Blackie put aside the script he intended to use on his radio program that night and wrote a new one about the pitiful condition of the old circus queen. He wound up the broadcast by saying, "I do hope that someone will see that Gert gets a bit of cheer on Christmas Day."

Blackie barely left the microphone when he got a call from the manager of the Ritz-Carleton Hotel in Boston, saying he had a letter for Blackie and would the broadcaster come right over and pick it up. The letter contained five new ten-dollar bills and a note saying, "Just heard your broadcast about old Gert Swasey. Please take the enclosed and give the old girl a Merry Christmas."

The next morning, Blackie and his assistant returned to Haverhill. He found a woman to do the cleaning and a registered nurse. He gave the latter $20 and she bought Gert warm woolen union suits, two cheap dresses, a nice red sweater, and "some other stuff."

A gang of boys was throwing snowballs through the broken windows so Blackie opened up his Speed Graphic. "If you fellows want to be famous and have your pictures in the papers," he said, "you've got to help." Blackie wrote that "they promised, posed, and pitched in with brooms, mops, and disinfectant. They scraped the walls and scrubbed the floor, set and puttied the missing windows, put new mantles on the gas burners, and when they knocked off for lunch, the old shack looked pretty good."

Cleaning Gert was the hard part. She kicked like a mule and swore like an old circus stake driver, but when her hair had been washed and rinsed several times, it came out soft and fluffy, like spun silver. Gert looked in the mirror and shouted, "Gawd Almighty! Is that me?"

While Gert was in the front room, the kitchen was undergoing a transformation. An oilcloth-covered table made its appearance, along with a white iron bed, two chairs, and some dishes from the five and dime. One of the boys brought in a small Christmas tree and carefully trimmed it with decorations.

"We tacked a bright red crepe paper bell to the sagging ceiling," Blackie continues, "and put oranges, apples, boxes of ribbon candy and some 'terbacca' on the table. Gert didn't understand what the excitement was all about, but she liked it. As we were leaving, a freckle-faced tyke provided the final and perfect touch. He dropped a tiny tiger kitten on Gert's lap."

From the street below, Gert's new friends heard the sound of Christmas carols and "in the hovel that was home to her, seventy-eight year old Gert Swasey sat peacefully in her rocking chair, stroking the purring kitten, puffing on her pipe, and, I presume (Blackie writes), dreaming of her days under the Big Top."

The Hidden Sweetheart

Following my mother's death, my father sorted through a box of ancient family tintypes she had kept. One picture so captivated him that he put it on his desk.

The century-old likeness portrayed a demure and winsome you woman in the costume of the 1850s, with wide leg-of-mutton sleeves and a lace collar. She looks appealingly out at the viewer, her hands clasped before her.

This was the only unidentified picture in the box. The young woman's life had probably ended before Dad's had begun, but that made no difference. She gave him pleasure and inspiration as he worked on his stories.

One night my father was working late. When he finally got up from his typewriter, the picture tumbled to the floor. As he picked it up, he noticed that the gilt frame was bent, and the brocade lining had worked loose. When he pulled on the lining, the picture fell out.

Under it was a small slip of paper, reading "taken in 1859," and "look under this paper." Underneath was another, hidden tintype of a young man. And under it, yet another surprise—a brief note in my mother's handwriting:

"Frances Drisko [the subject of the tintype] was born in Addison, Maine, in 1837. Addison is a small town near the rock-bound coast situated on Pleasant River. When she was 18, she married a young man who was several years older. Captain Dyer was the captain of a sailing vessel. She sailed with him to Santo Domingo on her honeymoon.

"Upon her return, he left her with his family and went back to sea. She didn't get along with her in-laws, and left. She came to Boston, very sad and quiet over her unhappy existence. When she was 37, she married again and had a beautiful, golden-haired little girl. That little girl was my mother.

"My grandmother was always reluctant to talk about her first marriage so I never knew more than the meager facts stated above. I had reason recently to clean out the house where she lived nearly 50 years with her second husband [the former Crane house in Quincy]. I came across this old daguerreotype which my mother had told me years before was my grandmother at 18.

"She looks much older in the picture. But if you are familiar with old daguerreotypes, you will agree that everyone did in those pictures. As I held the old picture in my hands, something seemed to urge me to lift the picture from its little frame and look underneath.

"As I lifted out the picture, I saw a small piece of paper written in my grandmother's handwriting. It said, "taken in 1859—look under this paper."

"With trembling fingers, I lifted out the paper. There was an old tintype of of a handsome young man that unquestionably was the young sea captain who went on his honeymoon with my grandmother so many years ago."

My father carefully replaced the notes and pictures. He wrote later that he wondered what my mother had thought of her discovery, and of how thoughtful it was of her to leave a written record for her family.

And, my father noted, he had known this demure miss with the crinolined dress. He had known her as a gentle, white-haired old lady who, when my father was courting my mother, used to sing hymns at the piano.

My mother's late brother, Arthur Curtis, remembered his grandmother and a few tales she told him of her family's coastal schooners. She mentioned once that she and her husband had sailed down to Boston in their schooner and a fierce argument had erupted between them while they were unloading lumber in Fort Point Channel.

At that moment, her parents sailed into the harbor in their schooner, on the way to South America. She quickly changed boats, and described to my uncle how the family later grew Maine vegetables in the schooner's cabin window boxes, off the South American coast.

Despite these conflicts with her first husband, the hidden picture and slip of paper seems to suggest a lingering affection for Captain Dyer that was never entirely extinguished.

The picture of Fannie Drisko sits today on my desk, and I cheerfully admit to a crush on this handsome great-grandmother of mine. Nor can I break the hold she still has on the present.

It's only a faded picture, but she left a memory powerful enough to be haunting today.

Dave's Premonition

When someone discusses premonitions, I think of an extraordinary incident experienced by my high-school buddy, Dave Schmidt. In the late 1940s, Dave and I drove tankers for Dairylea (the Dairymen's League of New York). We traveled from farm to farm, picking up raw milk and delivering it to different processing plants.

In those days trucking was a whole different world. Almost all trucks were underpowered, and there would be scrambles down one hill to get up another. The braking systems were terrible. My 1936 Ford used mechanical brakes reinforced with ineffective electrical "boosters." Dave's 1929 Brockway was little better.

There were no CBs or tape decks, so we "talked" with headlights. We regarded even an AM radio in the cab as a bit effete. Our air conditioning was a vent window or a cowl vent. There was much pride in being a careful and polite driver.

Most of our routes were through the mountains and hills of upstate New York and northern Vermont. The dirt and blacktop roads were narrow, curving and soft-shouldered. In the winter they knew neither plow nor sand.

Road salt was not in use back then, and I can remember spending three hours going through Albany one dark, icy winter morning, "burning" my way up several of that city's famous (to us) hills. This meant putting the truck in its lowest gear and letting the drive wheels spin until they had melted the ice down to the bare pavement. We might be several minutes in one spot.

On one such icy night, Dave, with a full load of milk, was taking a typical blacktop road through mountains on his way to Vermont. But the road wasn't black that night, it was white with unplowed snow and ice.

When I saw Dave in the terminal yard before his trip, he was his usual jovial self, blond, good-looking, always ready with a smile and a helping hand. I watched as he checked his tires, hoses, connections, lights, couplings—all the hundred and one things a good driver checks at each stop.

At the rear of his trailer, Dave brushed against the ladder leading to the top of the tanks. He jumped back with an exclamation of pain and surprise. Then he walked back, inspected the ladder, and finally touched it gingerly.

"That thing felt red-hot," he said in amazement. I walked over and touched it, but it seemed normal to me. Dave became uncharacteristically glum.

"This is not going to be a good run," he muttered.

I watched him pull slowly out of the yard, the yellow lights on his truck boring hopefully into the darkness, the red running lights on the tank trailer following. Then it was my turn to get ready.

I didn't see Dave again for another week, and then I noticed his rig first. The ladder on the rear had been shorn off. I walked around the back of his truck in amazement, feeling the jagged metal stumps. Dave walked by with the yard supervisor.

"Tell you about it tonight," he said to me as they went by.

"Remember that premonition I had just before the run?" he said to me later at the Launcelot, a popular truckers' hangout.

"Yep," I replied. "What happened to the ladder?"

"Well, about an hour after I left the terminal, I was in the mountains. It was pretty icy, and I was being extra careful, or so

I thought. You know that road, the two-lane downgrade heading into Vermont where you lost your brakes in the '41 Buick?

"I was pretty well geared down, nosing around the curves, and trying not to go over the edge. Slippery? You'd better believe it. I don't think I could have walked on that road, and here I was, with a full load and in low gear.

"About halfway down, I looked in the mirror on the cab door, and I saw some running lights coming up fast behind me in the other lane. Some idiot is trying to pass me! The road is barely wide enough for my truck, and here is some clown trying to pass me downhill on ice.

"I gritted my teeth and hung on, not even daring to look at him. finally I did look back, and he was still there, only closer. Then it hit me. That was my *trailer* coming sideways behind me, and I was about to jackknife over the edge."

At this point, I became aware that the jukebox had stopped and that there wasn't a sound in the crowded bar. Everyone there was a trucker, and knew there was only one thing Dave could have done. He took a swallow of his beer and continued.

"I got that thing into a higher gear and stomped on it," he said. "Eventually the tractor pulled ahead and got the trailer straight. I was now out of *that* jam, but I was going like hell on an icy, curving, narrow road with a full load and a sheer drop into space on my right.

"I tapped the trailer brakes very lightly to slow down, but nothing happened. I tried again, a little harder. Nothing. I stomped on them. Nothing. I had lost the brakes, probably snapping the hose when the trailer started to jackknife. I tried to gear down again, but I was going too fast. I was also sliding all over the place.

"I had about another four or five miles of mountain to go with two hairpin curves. I could see the foot of the mountain far ahead, and the place where the road crossed the railroad tracks at the bottom. And guess what? There was a long freight coming toward the crossing."

Someone's elbow slipped as he leaned forward to hear.

Dave continued, "If I speeded up to try to beat the train to the crossing, I would probably skid over the side. If I didn't, I was certainly going to crash into the side of the train. My only chance was to try to beat the train to the crossing."

So Dave began his race for life.

It didn't take much imagination for those of us who drove those mountain roads to picture the old rig, skidding down the steep grades, yellow headlights bobbing in the darkness, the trailer swaying, the skidding across the narrow roadway, the hesitation and then recovery at the brink of oblivion.

Dave made it to the foot of the mountain with a combination of extraordinary skill and luck. The crossing was a few hundred feet ahead, running across the approach to a valley.

The rapidly approaching train was also going fast. Perhaps the engineer was trying to beat the truck to the crossing, because the train whistle was shrieking continuously. It seemed certain the train and the truck would collide, and Dave confessed that he shut his eyes at the moment of impact.

But there was no impact. Dave just made it across the tracks. It took him a long time to bring the brakeless rig to to a stop on the other side. When it finally came to a halt, Dave shakily left the cab and breathed deeply in relief as he walked down the side of the tanker. When he reached the back, he looked up.

The train had torn off the rear ladder.

Dungeon Rock

As you walk through Lynn Woods Reservation in Massachusetts, you shed three centuries of nicks from Father Time's scythe. In this largest city-owned park in the United States, time has wrought few changes since the 1600s. The area is covered with virgin forest, Colonial wolf traps, stagecoach roads, and the cellar holes of some of our earliest settlers.

It's a lonely, frozen spot of time in a world that has reached for and touched on the moon. But you are not really alone in these Lynn woods. That whispering, sighing wind nudging the treetops tells you of a ghostly cave and pirate's treasure, entombed in Dungeon Rock, just minutes from hustling Boston.

Dungeon Rock is the site of a vast tunnel with foul, dripping walls. It was hand dug through solid rock, a foot a month, by two men trying to reach a treasure chamber containing gold, jewels, and the records of a lost civilization.

One evening in the spring of 1658, a black-hulled ship, flying no flag, silently entered Saugus Bay and dropped anchor. A small boat was put over the side the four men scrambled aboard. Nervous eyes peered from the shore and soon word spread through the early settlement. Pirates!

The four strangers rowed briskly up the Saugus River and landed on a wooded shore about a mile from their mysterious ship and disappeared into the heavy forest.

Although furtive eyes from among the settlers maintained a watch, the black ship slipped away undetected during the night.

The next day, a note was found near the entrance of the Saugus Iron Works. It requested a quantity of shackles, handcuffs, hatchets, and other iron implements, to be hidden in a secluded spot in the woods. In return, an equal value of silver would be found in their place.

The pirates—for no one doubted that they wrote the note—received the goods for which they paid generously as promised.

The fugitives found an isolated area near Saugus, a deep and narrow valley shut in on two sides by rock cliffs, and shrouded from view on the other sides by a dense forest of hemlocks, cedars and pines. The built a small hut and dug a well and planted a garden.

By climbing almost perpendicular steps on the eastern side, they could search the waters of the bay to the south, along with a considerable portion of the surrounding country.

Four evil men were sheltered in an Eden, an area known for centuries after as Pirates' Glen. Later, greedy men would dig for money supposedly buried there. None was ever found.

As ideal as the pirates' spot was, the fearful curiosity of the local settlers led to discovery, and word soon leaked to British authorities. A king's cruiser appeared, and an armed party captured three of the men. They were taken back to England.

The fourth man escaped, scrambling and clawing his way over rocks and through heavy underbrush to a cave, about two miles northward in the Lynn woods. The surviving pirate was named Thomas Veal.

Legend says the cave was connected to a large chamber where the pirates had salted away much of their plunder. It was here that Veal set up housekeeping and established himself in the unlikely occupation of shoemaker. He also made occasional trips to town to buy food. Why was he now accepted by the formerly fearful townspeople? On that point the legend is silent.

One of the townsfolk was an alcoholic woodchopper named Joel Dunn. None too bright, not too brave, he was nevertheless respected after a fashion by his fellow citizens as a hard worker and truthful, when sober.

One day Dunn was hard at work in the forest, cutting and quartering logs for firewood. In the course of the afternoon, feeling the effects of a muggy and warm day, he stopped to sit on a stump and eat his lunch.

As he took refreshing gulps from a stone jug, he reflected on the disappearance that week of a young Lynn girl. He also wondered about the man he had seen darting from tree to tree that morning. Could it have been the pirate Veal? The man lived under the spot now known as Dungeon Rock, and most people, including Dunn, gave his cave a wide berth.

Further thoughts were jarred by thunder in the distance. Looking up, Dunn noticed a yellowish cast to the sky. The air was unusually heavy and oppressive. The woodchopper decided to return home before the storm broke.

Shouldering his axe and carrying his empty jug, Dunn started off toward Pine Hill, the lonely spot in the forest where he made his home. Gusts of wind and rain swept through the valley. Bracing himself against the blasts of pelting rain, Dunn struggled homeward. Then he saw the man again. It was Veal, and the woodchopper decided to follow him.

The man made his way through marshes and briers and thickly wooded areas, and over glacial rock piles. Snatches of a sea chantey came back to Dunn, for the pirate seemed to enjoy the tempest. finally, the commanding elevation of the rock loomed near, and as Veal entered his cave, he spotted Dunn.

"Come in, bowlegs, come in," he cried. "Have a care for yourself. It rains, and chills may catch you."

As fearful as he was of the pirate, Dunn's fear of the storm was stronger. He entered, leaving the elements howling behind him.

Dunn found himself in a subterranean opening beneath the main body of rock. It was dark until the pirate lit a pine knot, and then the woodchopper saw a rough table, tree stumps used as chairs, and a shoemaker's bench.

Perhaps knowing Dunn's reputation for drink, the pirate asked for a swallow from the stone jug. Alas, it was empty, and Veal's features darkened.

"Get you gone, then," he snarled. "The lightning will light your way. Go now. The sooner you show me your heels, the better for you."

Scowling, Veal then forced his body, with an effort, through a narrow crevice leading to an inner compartment.

Emboldened by his host's absence, Dunn paused a moment to to look at the table. Among broken dishes, a rusty knife, a hatchet and other implements, he spotted a jeweled ring. He took it and slipped it on his finger.

The storm grew. Outside, birds uttered fearful calls. Inside, rocks fell from the roof of the cave. Dunn stood rooted, afraid to leave yet afraid to stay. The Veal reappeared from the inner room.

He advanced on Dunn with an upraised cutlass, roaring, "Did I not bid you begone? A minute more and you and your head will part company. Begone!"

At that moment, a sudden, rumbling roar came and the rock floor shuddered and slid underneath their feet. A series of deep growls came to their ears as deep beneath them rock ground against rock. A sudden violent movement flung Dunn from the cave.

Dunn was knocked out, and remained unconscious until he was shaken awake the next morning by another woodsman. The pirate's cave had collapsed, and the rock cliff was strewn with fallen trees, churned up earth and giant rock fragments. The famous New England earthquake of 1658 had sealed up the infamous Veal; hence, the name Dungeon Rock.

On his finger Dunn still wore the ring he had taken from Veal's table the night before. It was later identified as belonging to the missing girl.

Dunn reported his adventure to the authorities in Colonial Lynn. Here are excerpts from their official commentary:

These words did make much talke. They did holde loell Dun to be one not given to lying. But hee was given to another wickedness which doth sometimes bring up strange phantasies. Manie do think that these wonders be ye devill his doings ... ye devill first comeing in ye shape of a rattlesnake, and after, as hath been related.

Butt to me it seemeth likelie yat all fell outd from ye disorder of drinke ... We doubt nott yat loell did abide in ye woodes all ye night ... in which ye dreadful earthquake did appear.

Exit Joel Dunn, and enter the legend of Dungeon Rock. For the following two centuries, the winds blew and shrieked over the rock. Two hundred years of dust and debris collected on the curious outcropping. The legend faded.

IN 1854, a believer came to Dungeon Rock. He would devote his life to the belief he had in pirate Thomas Veal, the reputed treasure, and the earthquake. His was the faith that would move rocks, if not mountains.

Hiram Marble, born in Charleton, Massachusetts, in 1803, described himself as a hellion in his youth. He was "straightened out," as he claimed, by his faith in spiritualism—a religious philosophy of great influence in the nineteenth century.

Marble's first contact with the spirit world came as the result of a youthful visit to a spiritualist. While staying with a relative in a town near Lynn, he suffered an attack of cholera. The spiritualist, identified only as Madame Y, accurately described his illness and then went on to foretell his future.

"You will dig for pirate's treasure," she said, "and you will find ... "

"A bugbear," he said, laughing.

"The pirate himself, sir, or rather what is left of him, and a treasure with him."

"That is encouraging," he replied with youthful cynicism. "Can you tell me where this money lies?"

"It is somewhere by the seaside, I think," she answered. "Less than twenty miles from Boston."

Later he told three of his young companions about his visit to Madame Y, and they all laughed. One asked what was the most outlandish thing she told him.

"That I should go digging for money," Marble replied.

"Where?" his friend asked.

Marble laughed again at the thoughtful look on his friend's face.

"Within twenty miles of Boston, but she not give me an exact location. She ran out of steam before she got that far."

"I bet it's down in Lynn," replied the friend, and told Marble the story of Dungeon Rock.

Soon after, still feeling ill, Marble consulted a physician, who advised him to spend some time at the seaside for his health. "Everything seemed to point" Marble toward Lynn, he said later, and he decided to go for ten days and seek the treasure. The ten days extended into a lifetime.

After checking into the Thomas Veal story, and investigating Dungeon Rock, Marble bought the surrounding land, called Dungeon Pasture, in 1854 from the City of Lynn.

The treasure was his primary objective, but the moody beauty of the spot also moved Marble to plan a park there for posterity: an area with wooded paths and roads, to be constructed with the proceeds of the recovered treasure.

Marble began to drill his passage through the solid rock, hoping to locate Veal's buried treasure room. He worked under the guidance of "spirits," who spoke through the mortal form of a local medium. The spirit of Veal, apparently mellowed after many years, was especially helpful.

Hiram Marble was continually encouraged by the mediums, with messages, descriptions of the treasure, and faith.

At one point, early in the process of excavation, the first clairvoyant he consulted told Marble that within a certain number of hours he would find something to encourage him.

Four days later, an ancient-looking rusty sword with a leather-bound hilt and a brass scabbard were found in a large seam in the rock. Soon after exposure to the air, the leather on the handle crumbled away, and the thick blue mold on the brass began to wear off.

Despite his supernatural guidance, Hiram Marble made several false starts on the tunneling. Each time messages from the "spirits" hastened to correct him, and he would begin anew.

Eventually the tunnel was driven forward and downward 200 feet, but so full of curves that a modern-day explorer soon loses all sense of direction. The effort expended was enormous. It took thirty days to bore a single foot of the seven-foot-square passage. The rock is extremely hard porphyry, and every blast hole had to be laboriously drilled by hand, a fraction of an inch at a time.

Blasting was dangerous. Every charge of black powder was tamped down, and then lit with a crude fuse. Bucket after bucket of broken stone was carried up the long slope and dumped into a growing pile outside.

When Marble grew discouraged, another spirit message would push him on. Several of the messages have survived.

"My dear charge," began one, allegedly from Veal, in answer to a request from Marble for directions, "you solicit me or Captain Harris [the captain of the pirate band] to advise you as to what to do next ... As to the course, you are in the right direction, at present. You have one more curve to make before you take the course that leads to the cave ... Cheer up, Marble, we are with you and doing all we can. Your guide, TOM VEAL."

Only one more curve—another few feet to be removed a chip at a time, a foot a month, gnawed at by the gnarled hands of a man sustained by belief and hope. But there were many such curves. Marble labored on his twisting course for fourteen long years, forgetting all but the rock that lay before him, and the treasure that lay behind it.

Then, on November 10, 1868, death more kindly that the gossipy spirits, released the bruised and battered fingers from their toil.

When Hiram Marble died, leaving his son an erratic, weaving 135-foot tunnel as a monument to faith, Edwin Marble continued the task with even greater vigor.

As his father had been encouraged by the "spirits" of Veal and others, Edwin received "spirit" messages from his father. One of these spirit appearances of Hiram Marble was described in great detail by a witness. According to the witness, Marble's ghost described, in hollow, ringing tones, the appearance of the treasure cave in detail for the benefit of the struggling Edwin, still progressing a foot a month:

"Imagine a large room with irregular sides, nearly approaching an oval form. On the sides are suspended suits of armor, belonging to different nations. Six large chests are filled with gold and silver bars, vases, pitchers, and other utensils of solid gold, and hanging on the edge of the shelves are swords, with diamond-studded hilts, and many other implements of very costly and valuable character.

"Imagine a large Spanish sideboard. It holds a great portion of the archives, with other papers, public and private, belonging to a race which inhabited this continent before it was peopled by Indians. What light will be thrown on the history of the world thousands of years ago?

"And now may I say to you, my son, 'Go on! Persevere! Be not discouraged by what may seem to you to delay your final success.' "

So Edwin, thus encouraged by this and many other messages received through clairvoyants, chipped and blasted sixty-five more winding feet during the next dozen years.

When he died in 1880, all labor ceased, the familiar clang of metal on rock disappeared, and black powder blasts no longer shook the countryside.

Dungeon Rock has remained undisturbed for more than a century. It waits, with a dark, brooding silence, for the next intruder to try to penetrate its secrets.

Rain Unearths Submerged Behemoth

For nearly one hundred years, the second largest hand-hewn masonry structure ever created has lurked deep under the waters of a scenic spot near the New York/Connecticut border. Only the great pyramid in Egypt is larger.

This local hulk dominates the depths of Croton Reservoir, which supplies water for the thirsty inhabitants of New York City. I speak of the original Croton Dam, which was left intact, along with its stone pumphouse, and flooded over when the present dam was constructed in 1904.

Only once since then has this gigantic relic poked its dank and dripping hulk above the surface. This occurred in 1955 when it rose, black and ominous, in front of the startled gaze of onlookers.

The year 1955 could be called the "Year of Rain" in the Northeast. It poured day after day, as one storm followed another on a drenching treadmill. I had heard of bad flooding throughout the area, but such emergencies were remote from the Milford, Connecticut, farmhouse I shared on the seacoast with two friends.

At the time, the Norris family used their old home in Pembroke as a summer home. I often drove over from Milford, especially when no party was brewing at the farm.

So it was that, one bright summer day, I left Milford for Pembroke in my ocean-blue Chrysler New Yorker convertible, top down and radio on. I hadn't been listening to the radio earlier, so I had missed the flood warnings.

"This is going to be quite a trip," I thought, as I headed up the Wilbur Cross Parkway, intending to pick up Route 20 to the Massachusetts Turnpike, and then head south on old Route 128, through Braintree five Corners, and on to Pembroke.

Somewhere along the way—it may have been around Meriden—all the traffic was suddenly detoured onto the old two-lane blacktop roads. I recall a long line of Greyhound buses, trucks, and other cars snaking ahead slowly. I recall going through Pomfret.

Then, somehow, I made a wrong turn, and suddenly found myself all alone on one of the few Connecticut country roads I did not know. After a while, I came to a place where the road was under water, and for perhaps a half mile ahead, I could see nothing but raging water carrying large trees and other flotsam.

About a hundred feet in front of the car's wheels a huge barn, comically tilted, sailed past. I managed to turn around and retraced my route to the detour. There I rejoined the long line of traffic.

As night fell, I found myself back on my old friend, Route 6. The traffic had backtracked to Willimantic, where for once the noisy thread factory was silent, although it was completely lit up. Through the darkness, we approached a bridge on the two-lane road. The flood was raging around its supports, and the entire area was bright with emergency floodlights. The rushing water occasionally washed over and through the upstream railing, and the police were allowing one car at a time to dash across. I too made the dash, my heart in my throat.

It was now late at night as I approached Halifax on Route 106. As I swung over to Pond Street, near the ruins of the old amusement park, I found normally placid Robbins Pond (usually ten feet at its deepest) flooding the road.

I had to backtrack again, but at least I was home and knew the unmarked roads of the area. It had taken me thirteen hours to cover what was normally a four-hour drive.

The area of New York state bordering New England suffered as well. Croton Reservoir was filled to capacity and more, and water thundered over the spillways on Cornell Dam in Croton, now called Croton Dam. This continued day after day, eventually causing severe structural damage to the dam. To make repairs, it was necessary to drain the reservoir partially to lower the water level.

Thus it was that the formidable shape of the original dam appeared for the first time in more than a half century. There it was, black and threatening, like a disinterred corpse. A dead forest of tree stumps, the trees cut a hundred years before, sat on the exposed bottom.

Croton Reservoir is extraordinarily deep. I hadn't realized how deep until I saw the earlier dam so far below the level of the normal water surface.

Although the dripping old dam appeared to be dead, resourceful engineers brought it back to life, and got the spillways and machinery working again, all to substitute for the newer dam while it was being repaired.

The old dam, built in 1840, had formed a reservoir six miles long, and stored 500 million gallons of water in its day.

In 1989, while visiting the site, I found a massive construction project underway. Behind high cofferdams, workmen were building a filtration plant nearly at the base of the old dam, again submerged.

I was told that one of its old pumphouses would be restored as a tourist attraction. Located at the base of the old lookout area, it is made of large granite blocks. Although it has no roof, the metal railing inside and out is still intact, and the foundations and bolts for the old machinery are still visible.

For a moment, despite my Yankee roots, I was just another homesick New Yorker.

The Haunted Cross

My two sisters refuse to touch it, my daughters fear it, and my wife won't allow it in the house. I don't entirely disbelieve that this thing was responsible for three violent and unexplained deaths.

"It" is a Russian Eastern Orthodox cross that allegedly received the blessing of Grigori Efimovich Rasputin; a blessing that acts as a curse to those outside the Norris family. The cross has been an uneasy lodger with us for over half a century.

My father went to Russia in 1932 to conduct a crime survey for a national magazine chain. There weren't many Americans in Russia back then, so I suppose he was an early VIP. He was assigned an official state automobile—a Ford Model A—and an attractive guide, a Madame Olga.

Somewhere in the course of his travels through Russia, Dad acquired the cross and two icons. I don't know the details, but he was told that the cross had belonged to Rasputin and that it carried the monk's blessing.

I'm sure he considered this to be just tourist talk, and accepted the cross as an art object and nothing more. When he returned, my mother picked up the cross and studied the ugly oil painting on it of Christ, the Russian script, and the skull at the base of the cross. It looked like a grotesque parody of the crucifixion. She took an instant dislike to it; I never saw her handle it again, and it was the only object in the house that escaped her dustcloth.

The entire family, including the later additions, regarded the relic with unease. Not because of the alleged Rasputin connection, rather, because it was simply an unsavory thing to have around.

We moved from Quincy to White Plains, New York, in 1934, followed by several moves as we progressed from the latter city to Pembroke. Father always handled the cross during these moves, and it always hung on the wall of his study.

One day, a New York friend noticed the cross and was captivated by it. My father explained its history. Would he sell it? No, but he might give it away. My parents half-jokingly asked their friend to think it over. But he wanted the cross, and carried it away that evening.

A few weeks later, the usually cheerful friend glumly told my parents that he was on the verge of a nervous breakdown. He said he felt as though something was constantly pulling his car to the side of the road; that he had to fight the wheel. "There's nothing wrong with the car," he said, "isn't that crazy?"

Shortly after this conversation, the friend and his car were found in pieces scattered along a straight section of the two-lane road between White Plains and Purchase. Police could find no apparent cause for the crash.

The man's widow returned the cross, and it again hung silently over my father's desk. My parents were bothered more than they admitted and when a second friend displayed interest, they related the history of the cross without enthusiasm.

"The last person we gave it to died suddenly," said my mother.

"Damned strangely, too," added my father.

The man wanted it anyway. My parents were torn between their desire to get rid of the relic and concern for their friend.

But, after all, the idea of a haunted cross in the modern era of the 1930s did seem ridiculous. So they gave in.

I remember the man as a rugged health buff who did not smoke or drink. The eleven-inch cross seemed lost, clutched in his huge fist when he left the house. Several days later, my father returned from his job in New York City visibly shaken.

We children were banished from the kitchen while he held a terse, murmured conversation with mother. The man had been found that morning by his wife, still and cold in their bed. He looked as though he had been frightened to death. Officially, the death was ascribed to heart failure.

The cross came back again, and resumed its position above my father's desk. As the years passed, so did our shock over the two strange deaths. Dust and neglect gave the cross an aura of innocence. So it was given away a third time, and for a third time, death struck in a strange way. I don't know the details because I was away in the South Pacific at the time, and when I returned home, the subject was avoided. The cross returned, never to be given away again.

When my father died in 1971, the cross was above his desk, seeming benign and unobtrusive. But the family was not fooled. We did not want to give it away again, and neither my sisters nor my brother wanted anything to do with it. We decided to sell it as part of the estate.

In the meantime, I brought it home. My wife has a stubborn streak, reinforced by family talk about the cross. She refused to have it in our house. So it went, temporarily, into the glove compartment of our antique LaSalle. For years the car had been utterly dependable, but then little things began to plague it. finally, I asked the estate lawyer to hold the cross in his safe. He refused to do so unless a buyer showed up. finally we found one.

There was a small crowd in the lawyer's office, come to view the strange relic. People in the group commented on its great age, evil appearance, and the violent deaths associated with it. The buyer had not yet arrived when the lawyer excused himself to answer a phone call. He returned shortly with an odd expression on his face.

"You won't believe this," he told us, "but the buyer has just been injured in an auto accident while driving here."

The cross was not sold, and no other prospective buyers appeared. The cross is still in our family, and I suppose always will be. Apparently it just isn't meant to leave us. I wonder if the Russian nation would like it back—as a gift?

The Haunted Violin

It was a mournful tune, and that night it seemed even more so as we listened to the wavering notes produced by the sixty-one-year-old violinist. Townspeople claimed that this gaunt old gentleman could summon up the Devil—or something equally supernatural—at will on his ancient violin.

Seven of us were grouped in the editorial office of the weekly *Wareham Courier,* located on the bottom floor of an otherwise empty three-story building on Main Street in Wareham, Massachusetts.

We were awaiting the arrival of an angry spirit, to be summoned by the doleful tune being played on the ancient and possibly haunted violin.

Suddenly, a door slammed upstairs, and the violinist's fingers stiffened on the strings ...

The violinist was the late Harold Gordon Cudworth, of Wareham. He was playing "The Broken Melody," by the English cellist Van Biene, on a violin made around 1769 by Joseph Hornstainer (or Hornsteiner) of Mittenwald, Germany.

For more than twenty years, strange and unexplained events had occurred when this piece was played by Cudworth on this and other violins in his collection.

"The first time something odd happened," Cudworth told me, "I was playing 'The Broken Melody' in my mother's kitchen.

"All of a sudden there was a great rumbling sound by the sink. My mother called out, 'What was that?' I thought the noise might be from a water pipe, but it wasn't. Then the racket stopped. When I resumed playing, the noise started again.

"I didn't think too much of it at the time, but I do remember joking that the violin had something to do with the noise. Two weeks later I played 'The Broken Melody" again and heard the same rumble upstairs. I thought it was the cat until I saw her behind the stove.

"I am not superstitious," he continued, "but I began to wonder if there might be a connection."

Gordon Cudworth had a collection of violins which he had accumulated over the years. There were perhaps fifty violins in total, of which thirty to forty were, in his opinion, good. Two had inlays on their backs, and one, the Hornstainer, had 365 inlaid pieces.

"It was probably made for a member of the nobility," he explained.

Cudworth told me of more strange events concerning the old violin and the haunting pice of music.

"I used to play the violin two or three hours each evening," he said. "I appeared a lot on the radio and gave many public performances, and I had to practice constantly.

"One night, shortly after the kitchen incident, I had finished practicing in my room and was repairing a lamp. The doors leading from the room had old-fashioned latches on them. As I worked, one of the latches dropped loudly on the door leading to the attic. I looked up. It happened again.

"I felt a little shaken and left the room to go downstairs. I closed the door and was about halfway down the stairs when I heard a loud slam behind me. I looked back. The door was wide open."

Cudworth went on to say that on another night he came home, went upstairs, and was preparing to go to bed. Suddenly, the latch of the attic door slammed up and down four times, "as though someone was there and wanted me to know it." There was no one in the attic, but the door to the music cabinet was open. The top sheet of music inside was "The Broken Melody."

"Another time," said Cudworth, "I was giving lessons to a girl in New Bedford. One evening, after the lesson was over, the girl left, and her father asked me asked me if I would listen to him play, as he was just starting lessons himself with another instructor."

"I said, 'sure,' and we went up to the third floor. Well, as you may have guessed, he eventually asked me to play my violin, and soon I was playing 'The Broken Melody.' Suddenly there was a terrific rumble downstairs—just like the one I had been getting in my house."

" 'Who is shaking the front door so violently? Who could be there?' " asked the father. I stopped playing and the rumble stopped. Then I started again and so did the rumble, louder and more violently.

"I thought it would be wise to stop playing. The man is probably still wondering who tried to break in his front door. And so," laughed Cudworth, "I guess, am I."

Another time, Cudworth was tuning a piano for a woman in Rochester, Massachusetts. She knew he was an accomplished violinist, and asked him if he had brought his violin, and would he play for her. He played "The Broken Melody," but this time there were no rumbles, no doors opening, no latches being worked by unseen hands. But there was an effect.

"I don't know why," she told him afterward, "but I never felt so funny in all my life as when you played that tune. What was it, anyway?"

Once again, Cudworth played "The Broken Melody" in a Wareham home before a skeptical audience that had heard the story but did not believe it.

"That was the evening pictures and mirrors swung violently on the walls," Cudworth recalled with a smile. "They seemed a little relieved when I stopped playing."

On other occasions implements had flown about his kitchen when he played the tune on the old violin.

These events, whatever they were, had been going on for two decades when I met Cudworth. They were originally triggered when "The Broken Melody" was played on the Hornstainer violin. But toward the end of his life, Cudworth experienced similar reactions when he played the tune on any of the old violins in his collection.

Gordon Cudworth was a tall, modest, affable man. His musical talent was evident to his listeners, and backed by numerous press clippings. He never tried to explain the events that occurred; he simply said, "I just don't know."

This was the reason for the evening concert in the *Courier* office.

The door upstairs stopped slamming. Someone made a nervous joke about angry spirits, but no one made a move to investigate. The music continued uneventfully to its conclusion.

"As I told you before," Cudworth told the group, "sometimes nothing will happen—perhaps not until a day later, perhaps not at all."

"Will you play it again?" someone asked. He did. And a third time, while three volunteers sat upstairs.

Nothing unusual happened, and the party broke up reluctantly after thanking the old musician for his time and courtesy. Soon only I was left in the office, editing copy for the typesetters in Plymouth to set the next day. Night traffic hummed by. The police officer on his beat rounds tapped at the window and smiled, then walked on.

The footsteps began at the rear of the hall on the empty second floor. They were slow, determined, heavy—a man perhaps? They continued past the vacant rooms upstairs and stopped at the head of the stairs leading down to the office.

As they began to descend, I grabbed the twin-lens reflex camera and flung open the bottom door. The strobe unit filled the stairway with brilliant light.

There was nothing there.

A Ghost Phones for Help

My family has always had deep roots in Pembroke. My uncles, great-uncles, grandfathers, and other relatives seemed always to have lived there.

"Went to Pembroke today," my mother noted several times in her 1924 diary. She had visited Pembroke ever since she was a baby. Later, so would I.

Despite these connections, the Norris family did not live in the town as permanent residents until 1940.

At that time, we bought Fannie and Waldo Turner's old home on Brick Kiln Lane. The property consisted of three very beautiful acres of pines, oaks and holly trees, a large barn with attached garage, two or three chicken houses, and a very comfortable 1840s New England cottage with kitchen ell.

There was a two-hole outhouse on the property that had once belonged to the district school. It was lined with old Currier & Ives prints that I studied with interest, but they were common back then and considered of no value.

There was no electricity, and water was provided for the kitchen soapstone sink by a beautiful copper hand pump, which my mother polished with pride. I still have it.

The Pembroke house was always special to come home to, and we cherish our memories of it.

Eventually, we had electricity installed and Dad took over the barn as a place to write. Later, Charlie Turner combined the chicken houses into a studio, deep in the woods, and my father used it to write.

After my father died in 1971, I sorted through his many personal papers and came across notes telling of a ghostly visitor who came to him late one lonely night, while he was working in the barn.

He had labored steadily into the wee hours that night on a true detective story; he had bills and a deadline to meet. A writer's life is never easy.

Something disturbed him in the early morning hours, but he ignored it, unwilling to let anything to break his train of thought. A few moments later, it happened again. He looked up, annoyed.

It was one of two old crank phones mounted on the barn wall, and it was ringing—a shrill, strident noise in the night.

He got up reluctantly and picked up the receiver. A woman's voice, cultured but urgent, filled his ear.

"I've taken a fall, and I can't seem to get back on my feet. And I smell smoke. Could you come down and help me, please? And please do hurry. It seems that there is a fire here."

My father's faded notes record his astonishment at receiving this extraordinary plea for help, and at such an hour. He asked who was calling, and he noted a slight hesitation, as though in surprise, before the woman replied with some indignation, "Why, this is Abby Magoun. At the end of the street."

My father knew that Charlie and Fannie Turner, Corrine Winslow, and Andy and Mary Washburn lived on our end of the lane, so the woman must live on the other side of Schooset Street, near the river.

There was a click, and the line went dead.

One thing I remember most about prewar Pembroke is how pitch-black the nights were. It was an isolated farming community, with few streetlights, and people from Boston rarely ventured this far out.

Dad immediately left the barn and started the family Auburn. He slowly headed down to the North River end of Brick Kiln Lane, alert for any sign of flames or smoke. He passed the slumbering households of the Smiths, the Romines, the Lowes, the flynns and the Morses, and found himself in front of the Macy house at the end of the lane.

The darkness was complete. There was no sign of anything amiss. It was about two in the morning.

As he pondered the call, a kerosene lamp flickered into life inside the Macy house, and a figure emerged carrying a flashlight. Suddenly, a whiskered face appeared in the driver's side window, startling my father.

"Whatcha want?" the figure demanded, identifying himself as Captain "Doe" Macy, and my father explained his mission. Macy stared back at him in obvious disbelief.

"Used to be a Magoun family lived here on the river," he explained, pointing to an overgrown driveway near his barn. "House burned down twenty years ago. Used to be quite the shipbuilding family around here. Smart people. Woman died in that fire. Wasn't discovered until too late."

My father returned to the barn, deeply disturbed. He stood over his desk, thought for a moment, and went over to the telephone. He picked up the receiver. The line was dead.

He studied the instrument further. It was hanging from a nail. There were no dry cells. There were no wires. The phone had never been hooked up.

Lost in the Woods, a U. S. Mint

Except for one magnificent section, it doesn't look like much today. All that remains is a three-quarter-mile-long depression snaking through the Norton woods. Trees thrive in the shallow depression, and the only sounds are those of rustling leaves and the chatter of birds. But it wasn't always this quiet.

Remove the trees, dig out the depression and fill it with rushing water, listen for the roar of water hitting a giant water wheel and the rumbling of machinery, add the shouts of men, and you will get a feel for the bustle of a copper industry that affected a nation.

Once 200 men labored here to produce the planchets (blank metal disks to be stamped as coins) for the famous U. S. half-cent, as well as the copper that sheathed the bottoms of Massachusetts-built clipper ships and the copper tubing used in steam locomotives.

The roof of the Bristol County Courthouse in Taunton, made from Norton-manufactured copper, is a living example today of an industry that flourished a century ago.

But all that remains of Norton's glory days are the ruins of the copper works, which lie on land once owned by local historian Harry Burbank.

It is easy for Burbank to imagine how life was on this spot 140 years ago. He can visualize the canal water pouring over the huge water wheel, and hears the roar of the water as it rushes into the wheel pit. Smoke seems to belch from the tall stacks of the cupola furnaces, the machinery clanks over, and heavy ore wagons creak past, their drivers swearing at the oxen.

This imaginative sketch is aided by the ruins of the copper works as they appear today. Beneath the brooding trees and the stagnant water in the canal lurk copper and brass scrap, nuggets of gold and fire brick, slagged and coated with copper.

The first copper ore to arrive in Norton came from England as ballast in sailing ships. However, not enough came from this source to supply all the needs of Paul Revere & Sons in Canton, or the Crocker brothers' works in Norton and Taunton. Copper was not commercially mined in the United States until after the Civil War, so most of it was imported from Chile.

Until the Civil War, all the copper rolled in the Taunton and Norton plants was smelted from ore on the premises. Because of complaints about poisonous fumes, however, the smelting operation was forced to move to Rhode Island, where it remained until 1884.

The impressive canal system to run these operations, dug in the years 1835 to 1836, is magnificently preserved in the Norton woods. Water ran its three-quarter mile length from a mill pond, developing a twenty-foot head on its way—a great capacity in that area for those days—and turned the giant, twenty-one-foot-diameter overshot wheel. This source of power was far superior to the undershot and breast wheels common in the area then.

The wheel was made of extremely durable chestnut. Its timbers can still be seen at the spot where the wheel once rumbled and turned the early machinery.

Directly over the canal, a small and historic building housed a second water wheel, probably a breast-type, and two planchet presses. It was here that the blanks were pressed for U. S. large cents, among the most popular coins ever minted.

Before 1840, the copper works were manned by native Yankees, but by 1850, they had been largely replaced by newly arrived Irish immigrants. Among the legacies of the Irish is the remaining stonework on the canal walls, solidly constructed and well preserved.

In some areas, the stonework is fifteen feet high, perfectly straight and laid of close-fitting parallel flat stones that could withstand the pressure of the onrushing water.

Other ruins include eighteen-inch-square chestnut beams, and slag, green with copper, which covers the banks of the Wading River.

The copper industry in Norton began where the Wading River now passes under Route 140. The area, once filled with homes, was called Copperworks Village. Here, in 1795, on four and a half acres of land, a slitting mill was built to cut rolls of metal into sections. It burned in 1824, and was replaced the next year by a rolling mill, a cupola furnace and a refining furnace.

In 1826, William Crocker, Samuel Leonard, and George Crocker founded a company to manufacture and process copper. In 1831, three other Crocker brothers, Daniel Brewer, and Samuel Crandell incorporated the Taunton Copper Manufacturing Company.

The partners had a beginning capital fund of $250,000, a large fortune at a time when a skilled worker earned a dollar a week, and a dozen eggs cost a dime. Skilled craftsmen were recruited from England, and soon after the company began operations, Samuel Crocker, the head of the works, went to England to obtain the Muntz formula for a copper alloy considered the best for sheathing ships. The Taunton Company introduced the alloy to the United States.

The copper company was the financial basis of all Crocker brothers enterprises, which included the Bristol Bank formed in 1832, a railroad from Taunton to Mansfield built in 1835–36, the Old Colony Iron Works, founded in 1844, Taunton Locomotive Works, begun in 1847, the Taunton–Providence Turnpike, the Taunton–New Bedford Turnpike, and several textile companies, including one in Norton.

The company, dba Crocker Brothers, was a progressive one, and never stopped trying to improve itself. Acting on complaints of the acrid smoke from its plants, management added condensers to the cupola stacks to trap the zinc oxide in the smoke. The move was both popular and profitable—the company recovered $50 worth of zinc a day, and sold it for use as a paint pigment.

The company continued to prosper, even through the Panic of 1837. The company declared a dividend of $200 per share (obviously, there were not many shares), and announced that it would begin manufacturing copper tubing for locomotive engines. The company came to monopolize this market for years.

Production of the large-cent planchets also continued. They were produced in a finished state, with raised rims, ready for minting and final cleaning by the mint. From 1815 on, Crocker Brothers shipped sixty tons of planchets a year to the mint, receiving $50,000 in payment.

The company shipped the planchets in wooden kegs to the mint. After the coins were finished, the mint shipped them back in the same kegs, and Crocker Brothers distributed them to various banks.

In 1851, a high-water mark, ten million planchets were struck, the largest production year of large copper cents. Crocker Brothers continued to supply most of the copper used at the mint until the large cents and half cents were discontinued in 1857.

According to the official journal of the Rocks and Minerals Association, the Norton copper alloy was equal to that produced by Paul Revere, which had the qualities of a bearing metal. The oil-less bearing was probably originated about this time by a Taunton inventor, Isaac Babbitt, and has since been known as Babbitt Metal. It is a mixture of lead, zinc and tin, possibly with some other, rare metals.

finally, on October 12, 1884, the directors of the company authorized moving the Norton part of the business to the Weir section of Taunton. Silence replaced the noise of industry, and the forests reclaimed the land.

It was not the end of the company, however. Through mergers, the former Norton operation is now known as the Revere Copper and Brass Co.

The Tapping Ghost of Brick Kiln

While filming an account of the 1874 Costley-Hawkes murder case in Hanover, I took time out for a nostalgic side trip down Brick Kiln Lane in North Pembroke. The lane is bisected by Schooset Street. The upper portion has changed markedly since World War II; the lower part, with its sweeping salt marsh views, remains essentially the same.

I grew up on Brick Kiln Lane. Wherever my travels have taken me, this lovely country pathway has never been far from my mind. I thought it the most beautiful lane in the world, and it is still a contender for the title.

Regrettably, the 1712 Alden Briggs house at the end of the lane is no more. This gaunt, sturdy historic structure oversaw the building of the Boston Tea Party ship *Beaver* in the Brick Kiln shipyard. The remains of this shipyard later provided our boyhood diving board at the town landing.

When North Pembroke boasted a total 1940 population of 400, Brick Kiln Lane existed in a quite different world. The upper half of the lane, between Schooset Street and Route 3 (now Route 53), held very few houses. There was the home of Charlie and Fannie Turner on the Route 53 corner. Heading toward Schooset, this was followed by Corrine Wingate's bungalow, Mary and Andy Washburn's antique cape, and then our Civil-War-era New England homestead.

There were no houses on the river side of the upper lane. This vast area provided the track upon which we raced Bass Hall's blue and black 1931 Pontiac convertible, towing behind an assortment of old buggies someone had liberated from an abandoned barn. It was a secluded area of trees, clearings and blueberry bushes. Hamilton Drive, once a dirt road through the woods, leads to what was once the Smith's many-acred potato field.

Then little more than a high-crowned dirt path, with the thinnest of macadam coverings. Brick Kiln Lane was only one lane wide for its entire length, and it remains so today.

The lane holds memories of something besides pastoral images, though. I didn't recall just when I first heard taps and became aware of a very strange presence. This being, which showed itself as a small shadow moving over the surface of the lane, made a series of loud tapping sounds like someone with a wooden leg—tap, pause, tap, pause, tap, pause, tap …

The taps always came up from the river end of the lane. Very faint at first, then quite loud when just outside the house, and then fading into the distance toward Charlie and Fannie's house. I had heard, as one of the country tales that made the rounds in those days, that Charlie Turner's grandfather, Barker Turner, had run the Brick Kiln shipyard. This man had had a wooden leg. Could it be the specter of Barker Turner, traveling up from his shipyard to his house at the other end of the lane?

I must have listened to those taps several times a week for months before I investigated. Curiosity overcame me on a night with a full moon when it was almost as bright as daylight outside. My folks had long since retired for the night, and as the tapping approached, I scrambled out of my bed.

I arrived at the end of my driveway as the approaching taps, louder now that I was outside, cut through the crisp Pembroke air, mingle with the scents of pine and ocean. I walked down the middle of the lane toward the taps as they grew louder.

Without pause or any break in rhythm, and with a fleeting chill, they passed through me and receded behind my back. A shadow, the size of a basketball and moving at a normal walking pace, accompanied the steps. I turned around and caught up with the apparition. I passed through it again, with the same fleeting feeling of cold, so that the taps again approached behind me. I let them catch up. I strolled beside them. I passed through them at every angle, each time experiencing that tickling chill. I was utterly puzzled. There seemed to be no explanation.

The tapping passages continued throughout the years we lived on Brick Kiln Lane. I never mentioned them to my family; indeed, I felt sheepish about my "ghost." It wasn't until years later that I mentioned it to my sisters at a get-together in Connecticut.

"So you heard it too," said Josie. "It used to terrify Carol [our younger sister] and me night after night."

For perhaps the same reason, my sisters also had not mentioned the taps to the rest of the family. Did our parents in their bedroom at the back of the house also hear it? I never asked them. It seemed as though we each may have kept the same eerie secret.

Demon-Possessed Truck Screams in Death

Every occupation has its own aura of the unknown and boasts its own mysteries. An sometimes the most prosaic of occupations seems to slip the furthermost into the supernatural.

In 1950, I was one of many truck drivers working on Route 9 and 9W along the Hudson River. It was beautiful country, and driving a rig in that era was a prideful thing.

We lived and worked out of Croton-on-Hudson, New York. Our favorite watering hole was a tavern, now long gone, in Harmon, next to the train station.

We gathered here to relax and swap stories. I was the kid in the outfit, and too young to have my own tales, but I listened.

One night I found myself at the horseshoe-shaped bar listening to "Goodnight, Irene" with one ear and the stories of two veteran drivers with the other.

My truck—an ancient 1936 Ford—had mechanical brakes with electrical boosters. I might as well have dragged my shoes on the pavement. I used to roar down the steep hills in terror—standing on the unresponsive brake pedal, the transmission geared as low as it would go.

When I remarked one night that my truck had a mind of its own, one of the old-timers dryly remarked, "Or haunted, maybe?"

"Yeah," I grinned. "It's haunted all right."

"Don't laugh," the old trucker admonished. "Friend of mine had to kill a trailer back in '41. Claimed it was possessed by a demon. Happened up your way, near the Massachusetts/Connecticut line. And no way did that thing want to die."

"Haunted trailer?" I said. "C'mon."

"Well, we were kinda doubtful, too." he said. "But listen to the story and tell me what you think." Here is the old trucker's yarn:

The trailer had always acted erratically. New in 1937, it quickly developed continuous brake and electrical problems. It tended to wander for no discernable reason, and it accumulated far more shop time than any other piece of equipment.

Drivers on late-night hauls complained of howls, shrieks, moans and groans that followed the trailer's lonely progress through the dark. Because of its mechanical problems, and the spooky noises, few drivers wanted to pull it.

By 1941, the trailer had become a serious problem, but there was no valid reason to get rid of it.

Then the first death occurred. A driver who had the trailer that day pulled into a well-known Route 20 rest stop in Massachusetts, the Pike Diner, now gone. He turned off the engine, set the brakes, and went inside.

A few minutes later, he glanced out a window and saw a large group of people staring at the rear of the trailer. He went back outside.

A trailer is pulled by a tractor. It does not have its own power. But the back wheels of this trailer were slowly turning in the dirt, pulling the tractor, with it brakes locked, backwards.

As the puzzled driver stepped behind the rig, it suddenly lurched backwards and, with an unearthly howl, crushed him to death.

A month later, the same trailer was on Route 1 in Milford, Connecticut, headed for Bridgeport. Just as the truck started up from a red light, barely moving, the trailer slowly leaned over to the left and toppled over, carrying the tractor cab with it. The driver was thrown out and crushed beneath the rig.

The trailer was brought back to the terminal and parked in the back lot. No one was willing to haul it. One winter afternoon, a yard worker climbed into it to clean it out. As he did, the two rear doors slammed shut and locked with a clang. And then—the worker swore this was true—a demonic laugh filled the interior.

The worker was discovered and freed at quitting time, but later caught pneumonia and died—the third victim.

This all happened long before Stephen King thought up his car character Christine, but one driver became convinced that whether a demon possessed the trailer or not, it should be destroyed.

He discussed this with the night watchman, who shared a common dislike and vague fear of the trailer. Thus, one night, the driver drove through the gates with a powerful and unlit tractor, hooked up the trailer, and headed for the hills on a mission of destruction.

The trailer, like a live thing, seemed aware of what was happening. As the truck climbed into the hills on the twisting, two-lane blacktop, the trailer swayed back and forth. From time to time, of their own accord, the trailer's brakes engaged, only to let up with a shriek as the tractor dragged the locked tires across the pavement. The running lights flashed wildly, often glowing an unnatural angry red.

All the time, drowning out other sounds, came a cacophony of shrieks, howls, screams and groans. As he came over the crest of a hill and headed down the other side, the drive floored the accelerator.

The speeding truck roared down the curving mountain grade, its passage illuminated by its yellow headlights and a bright moon, the running lights flashing, the trailer swaying, its brakes periodically screeching, accompanied by unearthly wailing and screaming.

Halfway down the mountain, a large tree abutted the road at a sharp curve. The driver fought against powerful forces twisting the wheel as he approached the curve. *The trailer knew.*

Using brute strength, the driver scraped the side of the tractor against the tree and then abruptly cut the truck to the left to avoid plunging off the road.

The right front corner of the trailer struck the tree. The impact was followed by the usual sounds of a crash and torn metal, but overshadowed by an ear-splitting, shrill human-sounding scream as the violently disconnected trailer rolled over the side of the road and disintegrated in a series of shattering bounces to the bottom of the ravine.

The driver swore it was a death scream; that only something alive could express so much anguish and torment.

To this day, I don't know what to believe. What do you think?

New England's First Recorded Ghost

I am aware that ghosts and spirits form an important part of Indian folklore, and I particularly value this segment of my heritage. There is something heady in the belief that the Great Spirit manifests himself through nature. Perhaps rocks and trees do have spirits, and perhaps all wildlife are sisters and brothers.

And just maybe those early dawn mists rising from our lakes and ponds are indeed visiting spirits returning to the heavens from their nocturnal visits to earth.

It was different for the early English settlers. They had a written language rather than an oral tradition in which they recorded the visits of ghosts. This is the true story of what some call the first documented sighting of a ghost in America. It took place in Machiasport, Maine, in 1799.

Abner Blaisdel and his family began to hear knocking noises in their house on August 9 of that year. On the following January 2, Abner and his daughter heard a woman's voice coming from their cellar. The woman claimed to be Captain George Butler's dead wife. Her original name, she said, was Nelly Hooper. David Hooper, Nelly's father, lived about five miles from the Blaisdel home, so Abner sent for him.

David Hooper was a skeptical Yankee, according to my sources. But he was also curious, so he walked over, through a snowstorm, just to see what was going on. Abner explained that Nelly's ghost had been around the house for about five months, and he had no idea why she didn't choose her husband's house or her father's house instead.

The two men went into the cellar, and the voice was heard again. Old Mr. Hooper became an instant believer. He asked questions that only he or his daughter would know the answers to, and she answered to his complete satisfaction. David Hooper later said, "She gave such clear and irresistible tokens of her being the spirit of my daughter as gave me no less satisfaction than admiration and delight."

Paul Blaisdel, Abner's son, was the first to see Nelly Butler's ghost, in a field, shortly after her father's visit. He ran home terrified, reporting that as he was walking through the fields, he was chased by an apparition that "floated" behind him. The next night, the furious voice of Nelly was heard in the cellar. She gave Paul a tongue-lashing for not speaking to her in the field.

By February of 1800, Nelly had become famous in Machiasport and surrounding towns. Many people came to the house to see and hear her. And then, for four months, she disappeared, apparently frightened off by the crowds. But she returned in grand fashion in May 1800, before some twenty witnesses in Blaisdel's cellar.

None of my sources explain how it came to pass that twenty people were jammed into the cellar just as Nelly decided to reappear.

One witness described her as a "bright light." Another reported that she wore a shining white garment. Another, more astute female witness said, "At first the apparition was a mere mass of light. Then it grew into a personal form, about as tall as myself ... the glow of the apparition had a constant tremulous motion. At last, the personal form became shapeless, expanded in every way, and then vanished in a moment." Another person reported that Nelly's voice was shrill, but mild and pleasant.

Before the year drew to a close, more than one hundred people had seen or heard Nelly Butler's ghost and given sworn testimony to the local pastor, Rev. Cummings—who was upset with his flock. He did not believe in ghosts, and did not approve of their credulity. However, Nelly's talk was on religious topics, so Cummings had to take care in condemning her.

One statement made by Nelly, before many witnesses, was, "Although my body is consumed and turned to dust, my soul is as much alive as before I left my body."

Abner asked Nelly why she appeared in the cellar and not upstairs, where people could see her in more comfortable surroundings. She replied that she didn't want to frighten the children.

By now, Rev. Cummings was losing control of his parishioners. He decided to confront Abner Blaisdel, whom he believed to be responsible for the phony ghost.

Walking through the fields to Abner's house, Cummings experienced a revelation that would change his entire outlook on life. He saw a woman in a field, surrounded by a bright light. At first, her form was "no bigger than a toad," but she grew to normal size before his eyes.

"I was filled with genuine fear," he said later, "but my fear was connected with ineffable pleasure." Nelly didn't say a word, nor was their any need.

Rev. Cummings spent the rest of his life preaching around the countryside of the glories of life after death as experienced by Nelly Butler. And then he wrote a book about her experiences and her words of wisdom, all as witnessed by hundreds of people, and himself.

After showing herself to Rev. Cummings, Nelly made only one more appearance. Captain George Butler, Nelly's husband, reported that she appeared to him one night, and gave him a tongue-lashing for remarrying, after promising her on her deathbed that he would never marry another.

Enigma of the Wax Skull

Every once in a while I come across a true mystery so compelling and unusual that my perspective and objectivity are challenged by my enthusiasm. This is such a case. Although our investigation begins in New York State, the culprit is a New Englander. In following a crime without clues, we will let the old records tell us how a gifted detective brought the victim from her grave. We meet the first woman detective I have known, and what a marvel she is! We are angered by the tragic incompetence of a grand jury, and appalled by a terrible murder that took place in New Hampshire years later as a direct result of that grand jury's actions. Read on, as we unravel a fascinating "Enigma of the Wax Skull" mystery.

I have spent many happy days exploring the waters of the Hudson River and poking around the abandoned forts and mines that line the river. But I never encountered anything like the discovery two Rockland County boys made on April 13, 1922.

The boys had been toiling up the rugged cliffs of Cheesecock Mountain, about half a mile from Stony Point, New York, looking for trailing arbutus, when their attention was captured by the wild gyrations and excited calls of a large flock of crows above them. They decided to investigate whatever it was that had the crows in such an excited state.

finally, after a long, hard and dangerous climb further up the mountain, the arrived at a narrow ledge overlooking the beautiful Hudson. The birds circled and shrieked over something that gleamed white. There, in a careless heap, lay a bleached skeleton, picked clean by the crows.

The boys climbed back down the mountain and scampered home to report their find to their father, who happened to be the game warden for that section of Rockland County.

Warden Clarence Conklin investigated the scene, and immediately called Coroner William Stahlman. The skeleton turned out to be that of a woman, whose skull had been crushed.

Sheriff George Brown gave the find wide publicity, but for a while it appeared that it would be an unsolved crime. Then the residents of Tuxedo Park, a summer colony for the wealthy several miles distant, came to be disturbed by what they called a "lack of zeal of the rural police." Using their considerable political clout, they called upon the police commissioner of New York City, Richard Enright, for assistance.

He called in Mrs. Mary Hamilton, a renowned detective. She was the first woman to become a part of the New York police department, and at the time of the crime, the only woman. As a result of her successes in tracing runaway girls, she was assigned to the case of the mountain skeleton.

Mrs Hamilton immediately thought of one man who could help her the most. This was her former chief, Captain Grant Williams. His long experience of investigating skeletons had made him an expert in the field. He had also organized the Bureau for Unidentified Dead, making it an important investigatory tool; he had invented a system of laundry mark identification; and he had established the use of a card index for cataloging fingerprints. All these innovations had become standard police procedure, and gave him international fame.

Retired at the time, he was so intrigued by the case that he agreed to help Mrs. Hamilton, at his own expense. The two journeyed to Garnerville, a small town near Stony Point. There the skeleton reposed at an undertaker's. Captain Williams studied the remains, and made a series of deductions, disputing earlier findings by the coroner.

Captain Williams determined that the victim had been petite, about five feet tall and 100 pounds, about 25 years old, and had been dead for about seven months. She had had a slight curvature of the spine.

The killer had used a hammer to fracture her skull at the forehead, on the top, and at the left temple. He had attacked her at night, with her back turned, and he was left-handed.

Hamilton and Williams, along with other investigators, then climbed the mountain to the scene of the crime. They found a cleverly concealed cave there, consisting of an overhanging stone ledge, with walls of cinder blocks. A tall tree blocked the entrance.

The cave was furnished lavishly with blankets and rugs, even a bearskin, and with other homey comforts. Outside, the captain discovered a shallow, scooped-out grave. The body had lain on its side, its impression still visible on the ground. Nearby, Hamilton found a charred spot where the killer had burned the victim's clothes.

"Look for a claw hammer with its head chipped from breaking stones," Williams told the other searchers. "The killer used the same hammer to kill his victim that he used to open out the cave."

It was a perfect crime. There were no identifying marks, no incriminating clues. Everything had been carefully planned.

Back at the undertaker's in Garnerville, the two detectives looked over the remains of the victim. The more Williams looked, the more he wondered. ...

In 1916, Williams had astounded the world with a remarkable achievement. With clay, he had restored a head on the skull of a slain Italian laborer, enabling the victim to be identified. No one had ever thought such a feat was possible, but this man, untrained in anatomy, had done what scientists said couldn't be done.

Mrs. Hamilton urged the captain to repeat this work. Pointing to the young woman's broken skull, she said, "The only way to solve this vicious murder is to put that woman's face back on her skull. That's why I asked your help. I know you can do it. Go ahead."

People had called it luck when when the laborer's head was identified, but the captain said his reconstruction was no accident. Features exist in every skull, he told disbelievers. "The face is not lost. It is only invisible."

Williams brought the skull to a room at 330 West 15th Street in New York City, and began the reconstruction. Rubbing Vaseline on his fingers, he smeared some modeling clay on the skull. He spread it sparingly, smoothing the thin coating with his fingertips to the contour of the bone. He worked methodically, bringing out hidden indentations and contours. As he applied the clay, he felt the skin and muscles of his own face, occasionally adding more clay where his observation directed him.

On the side where the skull had rested on the ground, some skin had remained. As he covered this patch, some rough places appeared which he tried to scrape away. Then it occurred to him that they were pimples.

The cheeks became rounder and firmer as he filled in the hollows. Eventually the outlines of a human face emerged. The nose acquired an unexpected shape. There are four basic nose shapes, he had told reporters, and they are determined by the curve of the nasal bone as it comes from the forehead.

This particular nasal bone had a thick, knobbed end, so a decidedly uptilted nose evolved. It seemed out of place, crude, but the captain was not searching for beauty. He let the skull "map the course."

"Length of the nose from the bridge to the base," he had explained, "is determined by the roots of the teeth. Where they begin, the nose ends. Feel at the base of your nose and there you will touch the roots of your teeth.

"To tell whether eyes are bulging or deep-set, lay a pencil against the eyesocket slantwise down to the cheekbone. This leaves barely enough room for the eyelashes to brush against it.

"The pupils of the eyes are located by resting the pencil across the bridge of the nose. It covers both pupils. Hold a pencil from the cheekbone down to the jawbone. Allow a little more fullness, and you have the curve of the cheeks."

"Eyebrows begin on the inside corner of the eyesocket. Run your finger around the upper edge of the socket and see how they follow around until they thin down at the end.

"If the upper teeth protrude, there will be a full upper lip. If the bottom teeth recede, the lower lip will sink considerably. Prominent teeth below mean a full lower lip."

Regardless of all this, problems did crop up, one with the young woman's chin. One hammer blow had pushed the jawbone socket into an unnatural position. As he molded the chin, Williams noted that it assumed a long, lantern shape. It jutted out crookedly, giving the head a lopsided appearance.

But Williams stuck to the clues offered by the skull. Using only its bony frame as a guide, he labored on. Instead of the full and saucy lips typical of many young people, the lips emerged as narrow and thin.

Williams felt some force urging him on as the face emerged. He would later recall that he felt he was influenced by the departed spirit of the murdered girl.

finally stepping back from his nearly finished work, Williams noticed that the head seemed to have recaptured its vitality. He felt as though it were alive, and he gazed at the work, motionless.

"She was Irish," he said to himself. "That girl was Irish."

From that, he surmised that her eyes would have been blue, so he inserted blue glass eyes into the sockets. They peered back at him alertly from under lifelike lashes. Part of one eyebrow remained. Using it and the sockets as guides, Williams fashioned new ones from silk paper.

The girl's hair was actually her own, its recovery a bizarre story itself. For months, the body had lain on its side, imbedded in the soil. As the muscles beneath the scalp dried, the wind pulled the hair loose and removed it as cleanly as though she had been scalped. It was found it the woods, but the finders thought it was a wig.

When Williams came across the hair at the undertaker's, he turned to the Coroner's assistant.

"I am looking for a triangular piece of bone," he said. "It is missing from the skull here at the juncture of the right and left parietal and occipital."

"They didn't pick it up," replied the assistant. Williams looked back at the hair.

"But here it is," he exclaimed, pointing to the triangular bone adhering to the inside of the scalp. The he demonstrated how the sliver of bone fitted into the top of the skull like a puzzle piece.

It was easy to tell how the girl had worn her hair. It was long and flowing, and the locks were turned in under the ears. The back was done in a puff and the rusted hairpins still held it in place. Williams took the finished head, attached to a bust he had reconstructed, to a local hairdresser and asked her to wash, brush and restore the original hairdo.

The hairdresser unknowingly complied, but then nearly fainted when she discovered what she had been working on.

Williams careful efforts had created a face that peered in sulky bewilderment at the world it had left so violently. It was that of an Irish lass who looked impetuous and tempestuous. A young woman flush with life, but with a face misshapen and twisted, one side failing to match the other.

The nose was particularly unsuited to a girlish face. It had an outlandish, upturned tilt and a broad base. A colleague urged Williams to make it look more normal, but he demurred.

"I didn't make it this way," he said. "The nasal bone did. The nose must stay the way it is."

When the work was complete, Williams dipped the head in paraffin. The wax gave the flesh-colored clay a gloss to convey the transparency of skin. After resting from his 56 hours of continuous work, he took the head to Garnerville and left it in the Sheriff's office.

Meanwhile, Detective Mary Hamilton had been busy with her own angle of the investigation. She had determined that a Swedish woman had vanished from a neighboring town, an Italian girl had also disappeared, and that four girls, three black and one white, had been reported missing during the past year from the Letchworth Village Home for the Feebleminded, near

Thiells. This was about two miles from where the skeleton had been discovered.

Hamilton located the Italian girl, but the Swede and the missing white girl from the institution were unaccounted for. The superintendent of the home gave the name and address of a sister of the missing girl. She lived in Brooklyn.

Hamilton tracked the sister to her home, and Williams retrieved the head and brought it to the city. A macabre aspect of the investigation was about to be played out.

The two detectives took the head to 330 West 15th Street, which was where Detective Hamilton lived. They set the head on a table, behind a curtain, under a bright lamp.

On the night of May 3, 1922, only three weeks after the discovery of the skeleton, they invited the unfortunate sister over to discuss the missing girl. Unsuspecting, the woman came.

After a few routine questions, Williams asked the woman if she would know her sister if she saw her.

"Of course," came the reply.

"Then, who's this?" the detective asked, pulling aside the curtain and revealing the reconstructed head.

The poor woman nearly collapsed. "Lillian!" she cried.

Shaken, the woman then identified the head as her sister, Lillian White. Through tears, she gazed at the apparition, and then dissolved into bitter weeping.

Then she placed her hand on the hair, stroked it, and fainted.

A second sister was called in, but the detectives had learned a lesson from their callousness, and she was warned of what to expect. Even so, she gasped, horror-stricken, and then whispered, "Lillian!"

The two sisters told of the 24-year-old, Lillian. One of 17 children, she had spoken with a lisp, was nearsighted, and had been abused at home. Her drunken father demanded her wages so he could spend them on drink, and when she refused, he committed her to various institutions as mentally defective.

But she was naturally bright and cheerful, and she had been happy at the Letchworth institution. She had written enthusiastic letters to her sisters, hinting of wonderful news that would please them. Then, in the middle of September, her letters stopped. The sisters went to the home, but were told there only that Lillian had "run away."

In a town adjacent to Thiells, the persistent Hamilton located a maid named Emily Williams, on parole from the Letchworth institution. Shown the head, she cried out, "That's Lillian White! She was my best friend!"

This girl, who had been a roommate and confidant of the unfortunate Lillian White, told Mrs. Hamilton a sordid tale of passion and stealthy romance between Lillian and James Crawford, an attendant at the home.

Crawford was described as about 34, trim, of medium height, and well educated, seemingly above his $50 a month job as an attendant.

Twenty love notes were found among Lillian's effects, telling of meetings at the cave. Emily Williams told how the notes were passed while Lillian worked as a waitress at the home. Crawford told her he loved her, but Emily saw through his fast line. Even so, she couldn't convince Lillian that he was a phony.

Crawford was asked if he wrote the letters, but he was able to convince his interrogators by pointing out grammatical errors in them, and noting that they were signed "Joe." It was a clever bit of misdirection; his middle name was Joseph.

On March 14, a month before discovery of the skeleton, Crawford was arrested for the theft of $700 in cash, watches and other goods from the home. He was locked in a room, but escaped, taking the letters with him.

Two weeks before Crawford vanished, Ruby Howe, a nurse at the institution, resigned. She had come to work there just after Lillian disappeared. Reporters subsequently discovered that she and Crawford had married in Nyack, N.Y., on February 14.

Evidently, Crawford had been faced with a choice. Lillian had been pregnant, and her murder removed her forever as an obstacle to him.

Williams' estimates about Lillian turned out to be amazingly accurate. He was off only eight months on her age: her 24th birthday was May 31, 1922. In life, she had stood four feet nine inches tall, weighed 95 pounds, was stoop-shouldered, and suffered for years from acne.

In a locket in Lillian's records folder at the institution, Williams and Hamilton found a picture of the girl and a lock of her hair. A sullen face with a pug nose and crooked jaw stared out at the astonished detectives.

The match with the reconstructed head was perfect. The identification of the skeleton was positive. A swift solution appeared to be in sight.

But then hints of trouble surfaced. Apparently resentful of what they considered meddling by city police, Coroner Stahlman and Sheriff Brown refused to accept the identification. Brown also refused to consider Crawford a suspect, ignoring testimony about the letters, saying had only "run away."

A visit to the cave revealed that someone had clumsily attempted to destroy it and hide evidence. It also turned out that

Game Warden Conklin was the night watchman at Letchworth institution, and Deputy Sheriff Bonneau was resident engineer. An anonymous phone caller threatened Detective Hamilton. And word about the reconstruction leaked out, perhaps to tip off the murderer.

The district attorney ordered the head and skeleton impounded for immediate burial. Williams and Hamilton called in a lawyer, Dr. Anna Hochfelder. She had been instrumental in passage of the law establishing policewomen in New York, and was a firm friend of the department.

Attorney Hochfelder decided on a novel legal weapon. She filed a writ of habeas corpus for Lillian White, demanding her appearance in court, alive or dead. It was a plea without precedent.

She said that she and others were convinced that the skeleton and head were those of Lillian White. If the county authorities insisted that they were not, then they should be compelled to produce her, or show cause why they could not do so.

Justice Leander Faber of the Supreme Court in Brooklyn granted the unusual petition. But at the hearing, the superintendent of Letchworth testified that Lillian White had been admitted to his institution from Bedford Reformatory. That was all. The proceedings established only that a person known as Lillian White had legally existed and was last seen at Letchworth Village.

On May 27, jurisdiction over the case was shifted back to Rockland County, where a special term of the Supreme Court was held. A curious crowd gathered before the courthouse in Nyack. Never before had a dead woman been ordered to appear in court.

The star witness was the clay head, which now rested on the counsel table. It was not longer the carefully done work of Williams. The features had been badly damaged by crude efforts to destroy its likeness. This was the condition in which the district attorney had surrendered it.

Marred though it was, the grim-faced head stared at the thrilled crowd. Justice Arthur Thompkins sat on the bench. The head was placed so he could see it.

"This New York cop," stated District Attorney Lexow sarcastically, "this 'artist,' takes a bit of bone and a hank of hair and he would have you believe it is Lillian White. This 'genius' admits no previous study in anatomy, yet he is able to guarantee that this masterpiece once lived, even as you and I. He deserves great credit. Such a piece of art should be mounted in a museum."

Suave and dignified, the district attorney continued to make fun of the "figurehead." His sarcasm, according to a reporter, "aroused laughter. The case turned to comedy."

Mrs. Hamilton didn't think it was funny. She told the judge that the courtroom was not the place for levity, that a young woman had been hammered to death, and that the outrage should not go unpunished. The mood in the courtroom changed.

Then Williams recounted how he had reconstructed the face. He ended by telling the judge that he didn't know there was any such person as "Lillian White" when he reconstructed her head. Little, the superintendent, disputed this, saying that Williams had had a picture of Lillian when he was working on the head. Dental evidence was also disputed, and the testimony became heated.

Just then, the two sisters and a brother of Lillian White came into the courtroom. The judge stared at them.

"Are they relatives of Lillian White?" he asked. Assured that they were, he exclaimed, "Look at their noses! They all have the same nose as this head! That nose convinces me it's a family trait. I hereby declare the identification complete. I rule that this is the bona fide head of Lillian White!"

The judge's decision forced District Attorney Lexow and Sheriff Brown to seek out the killer. But they had delayed too long, and the trail was cold.

Williams located Ruby Howe's mother in Biddeford, Maine, and tracked the Crawfords to a rooming house in Portland. That night, Crawford went to a movie with his wife, but deserted her at intermission. He had escaped again.

Three years passed. On May 9, 1925, in Winthrop, Maine, near Lake Maranacook, a Mrs. Emma Towns was found in the woods, wounded, while her cottage blazed nearby. An intruder had shot her, she said, leaving her unconscious, and set fire to her home, and kidnapped her niece.

Posses were formed, and found the body of Aida Hayward, the niece, strangled and hidden between two mattresses in an abandoned cottage. The cottage had been leased to a Harry Kirby. From a group photo, a picture of Kirby was enlarge for a wanted poster distributed throughout New England.

A boardinghouse keeper in Newburyport, Massachusetts, recognized the picture in a newspaper as a man staying at her house. He was arrested. His wife, Mrs. Kirby, was located in Saco, Maine, and discovered to be the former Ruby Howe, the nurse who had married James Crawford. fingerprints identified the prisoner as Joseph Blunt, a burglar who had escaped from a

Brooklyn jail in 1919. He had also served a term in the Elmira, New York, Reformatory.

Williams questioned the man in Maine, who confessed to murdering Aida Hayward, but he never confessed to killing Lillian White. Before his trial, he committed suicide in jail by slashing his wrists with a razor blade.

Prompt indictment of Crawford by Rockland County authorities might have prevented the later crimes. But the head did serve its purpose. And the skull did speak from the grave.

The Bootlegger Ghosts

My father, a newspaper reporter in the 1920s and early 1930s, told me that there were an unusual number of haunted houses along the New England coast during Prohibition. Flashing blue lights, screams, wailing, and an occasional sheeted figure kept most of the curious at a distance.

Every so often, a venturesome newspaper editor would send a reporter out to investigate the spooks and many of these newsmen had some pretty hairy encounters with bootlegging "ghosts" that carried Tommy guns. This is the story of a strange, double-walled house off the Maine coast, once thought to be haunted.

Standing on the bridge linking Will's Gut to Bailey Island, and looking east, one gazes over Pole Island. A hermit by the name of John Darling lived here for a quarter of a century. Beyond that are the famous Cedar Ledges. According to Casco Bay tradition, a crevasse there yielded a pot of gold that raised the fortunes of a fisherman from poverty to wealth. Interesting waters, these.

But, back to Pole Island, which stands in the mouth of Quohog (local spelling) Bay. This is where, many years ago, Herb Beals defied the lightning, like Ajax of old, and in blasphemous language, defied God to harm him.

Beals, for whatever reason, stood in the doorway of his shack, with his hound dog looking out from between his legs, screaming his challenge and shaking his fist at the heavens.

"From the brassy ether," wrote a reporter, "came a roar of fearsome rumbles, then a single forked flame launched itself from the inky background. Beals and the dog lay crumpled bits of lifelessness on the doorstop."

For years after, Maine natives would point with awe at the splintered shack. Then other storms rolled by, and eventually a second bolt of lightning struck the shack, burning it to the ground and completing the vengeance of the Lord.

Close by Pole Island are the Elm Islands and Ragged Island. By the end of the 1920s, only the very oldest local fishermen of the lower bay would recall the strange and true story of the Ragged Island counterfeiters.

In the nineteenth century, the Maine coast islands were lonely and desolate, and attracted no one beyond the occasional fisherman. Ragged Island, with fifty acres, had had several owners. It didn't have much going for it, by contemporary standards. It lacked a good harbor, it was in the open Atlantic, and it was too far from the mainland to attract summer visitors.

Around 1893 three city-bred men came to Small Point and negotiated a long-term lease for Ragged Island. They returned two weeks later with a giant, black man. They arrived from Bath by team, bringing with them a large quantity of supplies. They bought a fishing boat to bring their supplies over to Ragged Island.

The also bought a large supply of lumber from a sawmill in Phippsburg, and engaged local fishermen to transport it to the island. Two more strangers, believed to have been carpenters from Portland, arrived and were taken to the island. Curious fishermen heard the sound of ax, hammer and saw, but when they attempted to land, they were warned off by the huge black man, who told them the island was closed to the public.

The carpenters left Ragged Island after two months of labor, but the three lessees remained. They were later joined by two attractive young women.

All the native Mainers knew was a building of some sort had been constructed. first they named the spot "Island of Mystery," and later, "Island of the Evil Name."

Frequently that summer, a two-masted, green-hulled schooner would drop anchor in the lee of Ragged Island. Curious fishermen thought that the small boat making repeated trips to the schooner carried wooden boxes. Generally, the schooner remained a whole day at the anchorage, then put off during the night. That way, no witnesses would be able to tell the direction in which she departed.

Every day, winter and summer, for three years, smoke drifted over the tops of the island trees as it escaped from the chimney of the mystery house. The big, black guard, always vigilant, kept all would-be intruders from the island, so activities there remained as much a mystery as ever, and of course rumors were born and grew grotesque.

About this time, New York and Boston papers printed stories with screaming headlines about the capture of part of a gang of counterfeiters. Their headquarters were thought to be located somewhere off the Maine coast.

Immediately after this, federal officers arrived at Small Point with one of the men who had leased the island. The others had escaped. Large amounts of counterfeit money had been found in New York, but no trace of the dies. In exchange for promises of leniency, the prisoner had agreed to disclose the base of operations and the location of the dies.

Apparently, through some sort of underworld network, those on Ragged Island heard of the capture in the city. They dismantled the plant and sailed away in the night. Their dies, with skillfully made intaglio designs (engraved below the surface) in obverse and reverse, together with many planchets of metal ready for stamping, had been wrapped in canvas and sunk near the mouth of the tiny harbor.

A strong rope secured the burlap bundle and a wooden buoy was attached to the free end. At dead low water, the buoy floated to within two feet of the surface, so there was little chance that anyone other than those looking for it would ever find the cache. Undoubtedly, the smugglers planned to return one day and retrieve it.

When the story about the counterfeiters came out, fishermen swarmed around Ragged Island. They found a solidly built fortress in the center of the island. On the outside the house seemed large, but inside the rooms were small, seeming out of proportion to the outside.

The ground floor was divided into a large workroom with a space at one side for a stove and a table for serving meals. Sleeping quarters were upstairs. Everything of value had been removed except for soapstone sinks and a quantity of piping to carry water. The site had been chosen to be close to a spring of ice-cold water, for which Ragged Island had always been noted. It was no doubt one of the reasons for selecting the island. The water was brought to the house by a hand pump.

A quantity of metal shavings and chips littered the floor of the workroom. The whole design was the result of a carefully planned program to produce counterfeit money, far from other people and nosy treasury officials. It had proved to be an excellent choice.

The house stood unmolested for a few years more, and many thought it haunted. Strange stories drifted to the mainland, and few ventured onto the island after dark. There were some petty thefts, but for some reason the local fishermen seemed to believe that the owners would return some day, and they respected the integrity of the property.

But no one returned. After a few years, the locals decided to assist nature in the demolition of the property. The sinks went first, then the water pipes, and then everything else moveable. Rumor had it that the sinks were doing duty and the pump still working near Small Point in the 1930s.

Everyone was surprised to find that the house had double walls. There was just enough space between them to allow a man to move sideways. These were probably secret storage places for the money while waiting for the schooner to come and take it away. There were moveable hidden panels in the walls that acted as doors.

Boatload after boatload of lumber was carried away by local fishing boats. All that was left of the counterfeiters' home a few years ago were the barely discernable overgrown rock foundations.

Almost no one today recalls the exciting past of Ragged Island. And one cannot help but wonder who the counterfeiters were and how their lives unfolded after they left Maine.

One can detest many types of criminals—armed robbers, murderers, and the like. But others, like bank robbers and counterfeiters, clever and skilled but not killers, give rise to a perhaps misplaced admiration.

The Mystery of the Missing Admiral

Somewhere in a forgotten Massachusetts south shore pasture, deep in the earth, lie two curiously intermingled skeletons. One is of a missing man, and he lies cradled within the rib cage of a horse. Neither skeleton will ever be recovered, save by accident, and upon this hangs a tale.

Many years ago a Navy admiral retired on his large and prosperous south shore farm. He was a man of great influence and fame.

I know nothing of his family, except that he had an extraordinarily beautiful and witty daughter who was the belle of a good part of the south shore.

One morning, on the way to one of his barns, the admiral abruptly disappeared. The search quickly spread from the south shore to the entire state, and then from all of New England to the entire country.

But the admiral had disappeared completely, without leaving the slightest trace.

finally, in the 1920s, a young lawyer, who would achieve fame years later in Plymouth County, answered a summons to the bedside of a dying old man.

"It's about the admiral," the old man wheezed. The young lawyer stiffened. The event had taken place many decades before his birth, but the disappearance was still remembered as one of the area's greatest unsolved mysteries.

"I killed him," the old man gasped. "What I tell you is in confidence and you must keep this to yourself. But I shall die soon and I must ease my mind of this burden.

"Back in 18—, I was one of the hired men on his farm. I had served in the Union Army and was young and full of hell. Like many of the other men, I was smitten with the admiral's daughter, and she felt the same way about me. We had met in secret a few times, and somehow her father found out about it.

"On the morning the admiral disappeared, a horse had died on one of the far pastures. We usually buried horses right where they died because of their size. However, for some reason, this horse was to be buried elsewhere. It was my job to load the horse on a farm wagon, using a block and tackle, and bury him that day.

"While I was doing some barn chores, the admiral came raging in. I'd never seen a man so angry and violent. He demanded I stop seeing his daughter. He got madder and madder and began punching me.

"I reacted without thinking, and stabbed him with a hayfork. He gasped, and died. I hid his body in the haymow. Then I brought the wagon into the barn, cut open the horse, and put his body inside. Nobody was around.

"I drove the wagon right past the search parties and buried the horse and admiral where I had been told to. It never occurred to anyone to check my load as I drove by.

"I married his daughter, and it was a good marriage, but the murder has been a load for me to bear all these years."

The old man died soon after telling his story to the young lawyer.

Many years later, the lawyer mentioned the story to my father, but he refused to give him names or details. He knew my father wrote mysteries, and thought the story would interest him.

Shortly before his death, I tracked down the lawyer and asked him to lunch. He said he would be delighted. Then I asked him about the story of the admiral and his daughter. He said he had never heard it. So he couldn't, or wouldn't comment on the mystery of the missing admiral.

The lawyer died before we could have the lunch, so his bit of south shore folklore will forever remain a mystery.

Boston's Hidden Streams

We were riding down Blackstone Street in Boston, and Dad, who had been a firebrand reporter in Boston during the Roaring Twenties, stirred in the front seat and grinned his mischievous grin.

"Ships used to sail down this street," he said.

"What do you mean?" I asked.

"Well, this is one of the thirty or so streams buried under Boston," he explained. I was hooked, as he knew I would be.

Many streams once sparkled under the skies of Colonial Boston, giving our ancestors fish, convenient waterways and pure drinking water. The Indians knew old Boston as "Mushawomuk," or the "Land of Living Fountains," but few Bostonians today are aware that the fountains ever existed.

The area was filled with scattered springs and numerous small rivers, with tributaries running into coves and small inland bays. Boston was also divided into several islands at high tide.

Most of the hills of old Boston were leveled, and that destroyed the old stream beds. Developers either filled in the beds or diverted the streams into sanitary sewers. The old streams didn't die without a struggle, however; they wander restlessly and hinder changes in ways that bedevil today's engineers.

In the Back Bay, houses and apartments stand on stilts, while tidewater seeps to a level of eight feet over what were once marshes next to the Old Mill Dam. Many of the sites of railroad terminals, warehouses, wharfs and business sections are built on filled land.

The Fort Point Channel alone remains to be completely filled in. It extends from Northern Avenue to Dorchester Avenue, and appears to have once included what is now called Roxbury Avenue. Maine schooners from my mother's family hauled lumber through these once-busy waterways.

* * * *

The early town of Boston totaled only 783 acres, and the peninsula was connected to Roxbury by a narrow neck of land. The neck was submerged at high tide by water flowing from South Cove and over the marshes where Back Bay is now.

The old shoreline of South Cove ran between Washington Street and Harrison Avenue, touching Washington at Kneeland. The site of South Station was under water. Continuing along Atlantic Avenue, the shoreline went as far as Belcher Lane, then northwest along what is now Broad Street to Batterymarch Street, and curved across Federal, Congress and North Streets. Water lapped against the present location of Post Office Square.

As one heads east, the shoreline followed Merchants Row to Dock Square. The North Cove of Mill Pond was in a curve near Charlestown Bridge. Sweeping over the spot now occupied by Massachusetts General Hospital, the shoreline continued past Boston Common and over the Public Garden through Park Square. From here, it followed Washington Street back to the neck.

The filling in of waterways leading in from the Old Mill Stream began early because of the increasing population. This was encouraged by the town fathers, who granted proprietary rights to the low watermark. This played upon the frugality of Yankee landowners who extended the low watermark by filling in their land. After several ships struck these pilings of logs and rocks, Governor Winthrop in 1634 ordered beacons placed on the obstacles.

There is now no trace of the most important and largest river in old Boston—Mill Creek. No ancient map shows it in its original state, although Winthrop described it thus: "North part of town was separated from the rest by a narrow stream which was cut through a neck of land by industry."

When Mill Pond was given to several colonists in 1643, permission was given to dig one or more trenches at Mill Creek. The trenches were bridged at Hanover and North Streets, and mills were erected at the west side of the creek and at either end of the causeway. A gristmill and a sawmill operated at the junction of Thatcher and Endicott Streets. There was even a chocolate mill nearby.

The first mill bridge over Hanover Street was rebuilt in 1686, and was subsequently replaced by a stone arch over which the pavement was extended in 1793. Mill Creek passed under a drawbridge at North Street. This bridge was later planked over when vessels no longer used the creek. This location, the division of the North and South Ends in the old days, was the scene of memorable battles between groups from the two parts of town. Later, the course of Mill Creek was altered to flow through what is now the lower part of Clinton Street.

Mill Creek finally became part of the Middlesex Canal Extension, incorporated in 1793. With stone walls, the creek was widened and deepened enough to allow sloops to pass through. It seems hard to believe today, because Mill Creek is now Blackstone Street.

* * * *

We know there were other rivers in old Boston, but records are either sketchy, unavailable or lost. Mention is made of one creek that ran into the heart of the old city, and terminated where Franklin and Federal Streets now meet.

A stream ran westerly through Liberty Square to Spring Lane. Its source was near the "Great Spring" which was near Governor Winthrop's home.

The intersection of Dover and Washington Streets—the site of the narrow part of Boston Neck—offers little evidence today to remind people of what it was like before reclamation began in 1708. Here sportsmen waded into the marshes to shoot waterfowl, and here, just outside the city gate, stood the gallows where many a pirate came to the end of his rope.

Almost all the famous springs have disappeared. Even the one used by the hermit Blackstone is gone. Blackstone's Spring is believed to have been on the side of Beacon Hill, near Louisburg Square. All the original shoreline is today buried deep under busy streets and crowded sidewalks. Where British soldiers embarked in small boats to begin their trek to Lexington and Concord, we have Park Square.

The first major enlargement of the city came in 1709–1710, when State Street was extended by the building of Long Wharf. Next, Mill Pond was filled in, between 1803 and 1863. South Cove began to disappear in 1806, and Great Cove was buried in 1825.

The largest fill-in job, of 570 acres, was the creation of the present Back Bay. The project took four years. It began in 1814, when permission was given, over vigorous protests, to dam the area.

The area became an open cesspool, extending from Beacon Street down to Roxbury Crossing. Between 1864 and 1894, this public nuisance was filled in, using great sums of money and much labor. This was the last major fill-in job in Boston, and will remain so until Fort Point Channel is filled in.

* * * *

Stony Brook has caused Boston engineers considerable anxiety. It has gone on wild frolics in the past, overrunning its banks. flooding cellars and spreading epidemics. The stream brought personal tragedy into the life of James Haley, former commissioner of the Boston Public Works Department.

"My aunt used to live by Whittier Street in the 1890s," Haley once told me. "It was an open brook at that time, and one year when it flooded a typhoid epidemic broke out. My aunt was one of the first victims."

Stony Brook was still unconquered as recently as 1950. Now it flows, unseen and unknown, under the city streets in a specially built concrete conduit. It flows under Roxbury Crossing, down under Tremont Street, and empties into the Charles River near the dam.

Bussey Brook in Jamaica Plain wends its way through the Arnold Arboretum in the Jamaica Way and disappears into the Stony Brook conduit near Forest Hills.

One unnamed stream, which has undermined city streets in the past, follows a natural course under Norway Street and then continues under Massachusetts Avenue to the bay.

Davenport Brook and Canterbury Branch are harnessed in Dorchester to prevent recurrences of their youthful escapades. Canterbury Branch is a part of Stony Brook and drains one third of the land area of Dorchester. It now runs tamely under the corridors of Boston City Hospital.

Until about 1930, a small geyser appeared occasionally on the Charles Street mall of Boston Common. It bubbled a foot or two into the air and covered an area of a square yard. This spring formerly flowed into Frog Pond. When the pond was surfaced with concrete, the course of the stream was changed, and it followed a layer of rock, which surfaced on the mall.

The conduits through which these old streams pass today will become part of Boston's future sewer system. This will eliminate much costly construction, but what a sad way to treat our ancestors' favorite trout streams.

Vermont's Vampire Scare

The winter of 1830 was a mild one in Vermont and a dusting of snow barely covered the bleak countryside. But where beauty rested lightly on the desolate fields of Woodstock, terror weighed heavily on the hearts of her natives.

The feeling would persist for some time to come—you see, there was a vampire loose.

How did a vampire, that scary creature from European folklore, ever find his way to the down-to-earth Yankees in the Vermont wilderness? And anyway, just what is a vampire?

Vampires infest the folklore of Slavic countries and the islands of Greece. Writings of the ancient Egyptians, Assyrians and Chinese tell of vampires, and there was a regular epidemic of them in twelfth-century England.

Various "authenticated" stories come from Hungary. No doubt, the Vermont scare originated in folklore brought from the old country by hardy but superstitious English settlers. The Woodstock scare itself possibly started from a fairly innocent event—a primitive attempt to stop a run of tuberculosis in a family. This answers our first question.

To answer the second, everyone knows (don't you?) that a vampire is the body of a dead person that arises from its grave in the dark of night to suck the blood from innocent sleepers. Between such nighttime forays, the vampire lies sleeping in its coffin.

Unfortunately, those bitten become vampires in turn. It is quite a chore to determine just who and where is a vampire.

(The Woodstock vampire was discovered by accident.) And once it is discovered, it takes a bit of doing to make a vampire feel unwelcome.

First, a wooden stake must be driven through its heart. This would likely deter you or me, but not necessarily a vampire. Sometimes the vampire must be dug up and burned to ashes. (This is what happened in Woodstock.)

The scientific climate of the 1830s was a curious mixture of old superstition tempered with new discoveries in medicine. The Vermont Medical College, located in Woodstock, was an institution of great repute and established principle. Its faculty of renowned doctors played a prominent role in the case.

Consumption, or tuberculosis as we know it today, was a great killer disease until recent times, and even now seems to be making a comeback. Although many say that heredity does not play a part in contracting it, the apparent tendency for it to run in some families has long been recognized.

So it was with the Corwin family of Woodstock. So many of that unfortunate family had died of consumption, or shown signs of it, that it is believed that the Corwins resorted to an ancient "cure," one which apparently had the sanction of the medical college, for the "cure" was carried out with the knowledge of notable men of the town.

The cure consisted of digging up the body of a person known to have died of consumption, removing the heart, and burning it to ashes. This was thought to stop the passing down of the disease in a family, and was the reason for exhuming the body of one of the Corwins six months after he died.

At any rate, the body was dug up, and the heart removed. If the party performing this deed expected to find the remains in an advanced state of decomposition, they were in for a horrifying surprise. The heart not only appeared to be well preserved, it was also apparently filled with fresh blood.

The gruesome object was hurriedly placed to one side, and the learned physicians of the medical college were notified in haste. They quickly arrived on the scene, and examined the heart and its contents.

There was no medical explanation for the state of preservation. The doctors present, all famous in this country and abroad, agreed unanimously that this was a positive case of vampirism. The big scare was on. Who would be next? frightened townspeople asked.

Farmers milked their cows, glancing apprehensively at the dark corners of their barns as their flickering kerosene lanterns case erratically moving shadows. Housewives fearfully locked their windows at night. The heart-stopping sight of an innocent bat was enough to initiate hasty flight. Children were required to play inside. Something had to be done, and done quickly.

To allay the fears of the public, it was decided to burn Corwin's heart in public on Woodstock Green. The selectmen of the town officiated at the ceremonies, accompanied by the staff of the medical college. They were, according to *Vermont Life Magazine,* "old men of renown, sound-minded fathers among the community, discreet, careful men."

The undecayed heart, still oozing apparently fresh blood, was placed in a large iron pot on the Woodstock Green and a roaring fire was built under it. Soon the fearsome object was reduced to ashes.

When the ceremonies were over, the remains were disposed of according to a precise ritual. A hole ten feet square and fifteen feet deep was dug and the pot and its ashy contents were carefully placed on the bottom. A block of solid granite, weighing seven tons and cut from Knox Ledge, was placed on top to anchor securely what little powdered vampire was left. The blood of a bullock was then spread over the disturbed earth. That final rite, it was believed, would end the vampire threat for all time. Well, almost all time, anyway.

In the meantime, Corwin's poor body was reburied in the Nathan Cushing Cemetery in Woodstock.

Eight or ten years later, some curiosity seekers dug into Woodstock Green, looking for the iron pot. When the reached the fifteen-foot depth, the diggers uncovered neither rock nor pot. All had disappeared. But, an old tale tells us, they did hear a roaring noise under the hole they had just dug, and they sniffed the odor of brimstone. Alarmed, they jumped out and rapidly refilled the hole. The ground was disturbed for several days thereafter, with rumblings, shakings, and occasional puffs of smoke breaking through the surface of the village green.

No one has sought the iron pot since.

How much of the story is true, and how much folklore? We don't know. The facts were reported as true in contemporary sources, but witnesses of the day did not have the advantage of today's scientific logic. Then again, we today are still ignorant in many areas.

The Nathan Cushing Cemetery in Woodstock exists today, but no Corwin tombstones remain. Was there ever such a family? The village green remains as lovely as ever, a favorite subject for artists and photographers, but the Vermont Medical College has long since faded from the scene.

One thing remains as true today as it did in 1830. The sudden, darting appearance of a bat in the dusk of a late afternoon milking will still startle the boldest Vermont dairy farmer.

Why? The residue of a long-ago fear?